The Coven

By

Cheryl Kennedy

W & B Publishers
USA

W & B Publishers

For information:
W & B Publishers
Post Office Box 193
Colfax, NC 27235
www.a-argusbooks.com

ISBN: 978-1-9429810-6-0
ISBN: 1-94298106-6

Book Cover designed by Dubya
Printed in the United States of America

Lewis Residence
Wells, Me – 1971

Were it not for the heavy rain beating against the attic's only window, or the scratching of the branches of a century old birch against the home's neglected exterior; six year old Eliza Lewis might have fallen asleep as her mother had intended her to do. Had she slept atop the musty straw-filled mattress that stunk of mildew and rotting fibers from years outside cushioning soft bottoms from the hard wooden planks of the porch swing; she might have never heard that which she was too young to hear even if she was separated by two floors and the locked door that held her prisoner. Unfortunately, the storm had moved in earlier than expected and despite her best efforts, she was far too frightened to sleep.

Each corner of the attic was occupied with elements guaranteed to give a young girl nightmares. In front of her to the right stood an old wooden floor mirror protected by a sheet that occasionally fluttered when a gust of wind forced its way through the ventilator, bringing it to life like a ghost from an old B-rated horror movie. To her left, a seemingly dark empty corner sent chills down her spine every time a car drove by casting eerie shadows that seemed to stretch their long claws in her direction. Behind her to the right she could hear the gnawing and scurrying of a family of mice, making a meal out of a pile of old clothes. Only her young mind envisioned a pack of hideous monsters smacking their lips and then scurrying about in search of their prey. The worst, however, came from the final corner. That corner she refused to look at. Were she braver she might have ventured over to discover the remnants of a scarecrow left over from past Halloweens, but her fear of the unknown kept her at bay. Only once she had snuck a peek just long enough to see a headless body dressed in dirty overalls.

A good mother would have taken her by the hand while she had familiarized herself with her surroundings; reassuring her she had nothing to fear. A good mother would have left the light on or perhaps let her bring her favorite doll to keep her company until she fell asleep. A good mother would have sat by her side, stroking her hair and humming a soothing lullaby; however Helena was anything but a good mother. A good mother would never lock her child away in an attic, even if it were for only one evening. Despite all her begging and pleading, her mother had insisted she would spend the night locked away while her sister, who was only four years older, was welcomed into the coven.

A small whimper escaped her lips as another round of thunder and lightning shook the house and lit up the evening sky, giving Eliza a glimpse of a pair of glass eyes belonging to a forgotten doll tucked inside a tower of boxes. The darkness had returned much too quickly for her young mind to comprehend what she had seen, so rather than retrieve the doll to comfort her, she forced herself to look away, imagining the eyes belonged to some sinister being planted by her mother to make sure she stayed put.

Down below her she could hear mumblings of "the sisterhood,", as her mother called them. Determined to rid her young mind of her terrifying surroundings, Eliza concentrated on the ceremony. Crawling on her hands and knees, she made her way to the closed door where she laid on her belly, peering through the slit at the bottom of the door. Although there was no light above the staircase leading up to the attic, she was able to make out a dim shaft of light coming from the second floor landing and was comforted by its presence.

Her fears and gentle sobbing had drowned out the arrival of the women, but she could now clearly recognize several of their voices. There was her mother, of course, leading the women in some sort of prayer; as well as Mrs. Putnam, her first grade teacher who's stern voice could be heard directing the women into a circle. For a moment Eliza wondered if perhaps she was going to tell the women a story, like she did when she told her and her classmates to sit in a circle, but then she heard Mrs. Pritchett, who worked at the library, instruct them to all join hands. As she listened she recognized Sarah Walcott's voice reciting some sort of rhyme. Sarah was older than her sister Anais. Sarah went to the big kid's school with her best friend, Celeste's half brother. If only Celeste were there to remind her they weren't babies anymore and tell her to be brave.

Eliza understood little about the sisterhood, partly because she had never been allowed to attend their parties, but mainly due to the fact that they were so secretive. Celeste's brother had teased them when he overheard the girls talking about joining the sisterhood when they grew up. According to Jeffrey the sisterhood was a club of witches. Neither Celeste nor Eliza believed him of course. After all, none of the women wore pointy hats or flew on broomsticks. Whatever the sisterhood was, they were determined to join in some day.

Outside the storm grew stronger, seemingly working in cadence with the activity below. As the rain continued to beat down on the patched roof, a steady stream of water began to trickle down from the ceiling above her; splashing loudly into an aluminum lobster pot placed there intentionally for the purpose of collecting rainwater.

As she repositioned herself, pressing her ear to the door, another bolt of lightning lit up the evening sky and sent a wave of pure terror through her trembling body. At the same time she felt the warm release of the contents of her small bladder, soaking her nightgown and the bare wood floor.

Scurrying back to the straw mattress, Eliza franticly looked around her for something to cover her lap. Maybe if she concentrated and squinted her eyes, she might find one of her sister's old nightgowns or perhaps a tee shirt that her mother forgot to throw away after her father died. An unexpected memory of her father tucking her into bed brought a lump to her throat and she squeezed back tears that threatened to be her undoing. Her father would never send her to the attic. If he were there now her mother would be in trouble for even suggesting it.

Downstairs the shrill screech of her sister forced her back to reality and she rushed back to the door, no longer concerned about her wet nightclothes. An eerie silence that seemed to stretch across time, was followed by another loud, more painful scream. Now she could hear her mother call out for her sister to be quiet as the other women began to chant. Desperate to come to her sibling's aid, Eliza searched the floor of the attic on hands and knees for anything she might use as a tool to unlock the door. Feeling around in the darkness, her hand grazed a rat as it made an attempt to scurry for cover. Immediately she drew back in horror, too frightened to move forward or crawl back to the safety of the small shaft of light.

To calm her nerves she counted to ten, as her sister had once told her to do whenever she got too excited or angry and it was just then that she spotted a small metal object jutting out from behind a stack of old magazines. More cautiously than before, she eased her way toward the object, making certain another critter didn't cross her path. Finally, she reached out and grabbed what turned out to be a pair of knitting needles attached to a ball of chewed up yarn. Tossing the yarn aside, she scrambled back to the door and set to work on the lock.

Although she could no longer hear the cries of her sister, the chanting increased in volume as well as tempo. As she struggled to unlock the door, the chanting suddenly stopped, leaving only the sound of her rapidly beating heart and her jagged breath. Removing the needle, Eliza peered through the keyhole. Once again she realized she was unable to see beyond the hallway and she resumed her efforts, determined to free herself from the makeshift prison.

Below, the women gathered around the young candidate, anointing her with oils as she swayed back and forth to the beat of an imaginary drum. Upon her otherwise naked body she wore a string of beads around her neck. On the palm of her hand she wore the brand of the blood sacrifice still dripping onto the floor. A candle symbolizing fire stood at the front of the circle, its yellow flame flickering in cadence with the slow moving circle.

Dressed in a long black robe, Helena entered the circle, making her presence known to all those around her by the removal of her hood. It was then that little Eliza silently made her way down the attic stairs onto the second floor landing. Carefully listening to make certain she wasn't heard, she proceeded down the hallway toward the main staircase. Aware that the old house with its creaky floorboards and echoing ceilings made it difficult to move about without alerting others, Eliza sat at the top of the stairs and waited for the chanting to resume. Every nerve in her body tingled with fear as she slowly made her way down the staircase one step at a time. Once she was safely at the bottom, she tiptoed toward the sitting room nervously checking left and right to make certain she wasn't spotted. From behind a large plant stand, she peered through the leaves of snake plant where she watched in silence as her sister's naked body was draped in a white gown and liquid was poured over her head. Unable to clearly see whether or not Anais was in pain, Eliza moved further into the room, unaware that her presence was now revealed.

Despite her insistence that Eliza not be present during the ritual, the child had disobeyed and for that Helena sought to punish her. Though her choices in regards to childrearing were anything but mainstream, Helena did the best she knew how. Her decision to lock Eliza away in the attic was one she made out of necessity, not choice. Every girl she knew old enough to babysit was either unable or unwilling to do so. The few women she was friendly with in the community were part of the sisterhood. Moving outside the circle, Helena then returned the hood to her head. Hiding her face she slowly made her way across the room where she pulled away a cloth exposing the birdcage housing a pair of parakeets belonging to Eliza and Anais. Originally she had planned to sacrifice Anais' bird as part of the ritual, but given Eliza's deliberate act of defiance, she reached into the cage and removed her beloved pet.

Eliza covered her mouth with her hands to suppress an audible gasp. What could her mother want with the tiny creature? The pet she had named Little Boy Blue had never hurt anyone and Mother herself had insisted the birds never leave their cage. Wiping away a steady stream of tears that clouded her vision, Eliza looked around her, hoping someone might step forward and stop whatever was about to happen; but all eyes remained focused on Anais.

Outside the circle, Helena held the tiny bird in one hand over an empty bowl. With her free hand she grasped a small knife and holding it like a pen she pressed it into the birds chest. As Eliza watched in shocked horror, her mother drained the lifeless bird of its blood. Before returning to the others she tossed the dead bird into a wastebasket, briefly looking at her daughter who had just witnessed the cruel and unforgivable act.

Whatever message Helena was trying to send to her daughter was lost in translation for Eliza was far too young and much too innocent to comprehend such cruelty.

Forgotten was the wellbeing of her sister, her sole reason for defying her mother in the first place. As quietly as she'd come, Eliza made her way back to the attic. She wouldn't see her mother dip her finger into the blood and draw a pentagram upon the foreheads of each member of the sister-hood. She wouldn't see the delight in her sister's eyes as they welcomed her into the coven. With her innocence shattered, she lay upon the musty mattress, vowing to make her mother pay for what she had done.

Chapter One

It had been nearly four years since Anais
had been inducted into the fold and not a day went
by that Eliza didn't relive the moment she lost her
innocence. Nearly every waking hour she had
fantasized of seeking vengeance for her helpless
pet whose life did her mother take so callously.
Neither her mother nor her sister attempted to
soothe her broken heart, in fact; no mention was
ever made of that fateful night. As soon as she was
old enough to read, Eliza spent countless hours
behind her bedroom door pouring over spell books
she snuck out of her mother's secret hiding place.

After that night things had returned to
normal, or as normal as possible in the home of a
High Priestess, and all except Eliza behaved as
though the entire event was nothing more than a
figment of a young child's imagination. Eliza had

approached her sister first, questioning whether or not she was okay.

After her initial look of confusion, Anais waved her away telling her she was fine and to get out of her room.

Next, Eliza had cautiously approached her mother, feeling out her mood with trivial questions about the upcoming weekend. When it appeared her mother was neither angry nor particularly talkative, Eliza asked if she could bury the bird in the backyard.

"Bury what bird, Eliza?" Helena asked.

Eliza stared at her mother with confusion. "Little Boy Blue."

"I have no idea what you're talking about. Run along now, Mommy has work to do."

Eliza left the room, afraid to anger her mother with further questions, and made a beeline for the sitting room. Transformed once more, nothing remained of the scene she had witnessed the previous night. Gone were the tall floor candleholders used to illuminate the otherwise dark room. Gone was the strange circle drawn in chalk in the center of the floor, marking the spot each member of the coven would stand. The table that had once held instruments intended for the ceremony now held only a bowl of plastic fruit and a stack of old magazines. Eliza made her way around the sofa searching in vain for the wastebasket that held her beloved pet, but it too was gone. As quickly as her little legs would take her she ran to the birdcage and pulled off its cover. There sitting upon the top perch was one green parakeet and one bright blue.

Was it possible that she had imagined the entire thing? Perhaps she had fallen asleep after all and dreamt the entire episode. It wasn't until later that day when she overheard her mother on the phone detailing how she replaced the dead bird, confident that young Eliza had learned a valuable lesson, that she realized how cruel her mother could be.

The manner in which she spoke so casually about killing the innocent creature made little Eliza's body quiver in fear. If only she hadn't heard the conversation…if she had continued to believe that the images burned in her mind were merely the nightmares of a scared child left alone in the dark; her life might have taken a different path.

After that, she secretly followed her mother about the house, watching her every move and plotting her revenge. Whenever her mother was occupied making dinner or doing chores she would sneak into her room and rifle through her drawers. Just what she was looking for she wasn't certain, but she was confident she would know when she found it. Several times her mother had questioned whether or not she had been going through her things, reminding Eliza her room was off limits; but the child would merely shake her head, insisting it wasn't her. On one occasion she had nearly been caught rifling through a box in the closet when her mother suddenly entered the room unexpectedly. If it wasn't for the fact her mother's closet really was such a mess, she might have been spotted when her mother reached in to retrieve a sweater hanging mere inches away from Eliza's head. Holding her breath, she remained still until she heard her mother's footsteps retreat down the stairs before slipping out of the closet and back to the safety of her own room.

It was the very next day when Eliza returned to the closet to continue her search that she had stumbled upon the secret inner closet. Being far too short to reach the upper shelf, she had retrieved a couple of old boxes from the back of the closet, piling one on top of the other.

Steadying herself, she reached for the shelf when the bottom box crumbled under her weight and sent her crashing against the back wall. The force of her fall against the plywood door had dislodged the eyehook used to secure it and she found herself sprawled out on her belly, face to face with the most horrifying artifacts she had ever seen. Luckily for Eliza, her mother was downstairs vacuuming; otherwise her scream would have most certainly given her away. Clasping her hands over her mouth to silence her scream, Eliza scrambled to right herself. Feeling cautiously around her, she located the tail of a pull chain switch and yanked with all her might. As her eyes adjusted to her surroundings she unconsciously held her breath.

At approximately six feet wide and five feet deep, the space was no bigger than their kitchen pantry. Against the left wall stood a small table draped in black cloth. Atop the table were the very instruments Eliza had witnessed her mother use during the ceremony. A long board was anchored to the back wall and served as a shelf to store a variety of herbs, incense, oils and candles as well as bowls, pouches and blades, some of the latter sheathed in leather cases. Below the shelf was a variety of masks, much too frightening for Eliza to take a closer look at.

Most terrifying of all however, were the skeletal remains of several small animals, amongst them her precious Little Boy Blue. Though not yet petrified, the tiny bird had been drained of his blood and was sealed inside a clear plastic bag. The once plump body, now nothing more than feather and bone. The smell of its rotting flesh made her gag and when she looked closer she could see maggots crawling in and out of its tiny body. Eliza brushed tears away with the back of her hand, as her vision grew more and more cloudy. As she lifted the bag, his feathers fell away, leaving only the grayish skin to protect its fragile bones and the sickening maggots.

Horrified, Eliza dropped the bird, gagging as its lifeless body hit the floor. Backing quickly out of the room, she grabbed what appeared to be an old family Bible before switching off the light and securing the door. Safely back in her room she examined the book more closely. The book was bound in leather and bore the Lewis family crest. Other than the family name, no other words were inscribed atop its cover. Along the side of the book were two metal locks, which Eliza set to work on, easily prying them open with the aid of a bobby pin. Taking a deep breath to steady her nerves and listening to make sure no one was coming, she gently opened the cover to reveal the inscription within. Written in beautiful script, no doubt by ink and quill were the words, " *Lewis Book of Shadows* ".

While the sisterhood met at least once a month, it rarely happened that her mother hosted the gatherings, so Eliza had little opportunity to witness their magic. Whenever possible, Eliza spent those nights at her friend Celeste's house. Although Jeffrey insisted that the girls stay in his sister's room and not bother him, it was still much better than being alone.

Now that Anais was a part of the group, Helena could no longer rely on her eldest daughter to watch over her, so the responsibility fell upon the other members of the coven to arrange sitters for those that needed tending to.

Aside from Celeste and Eliza there were three young boys that were too young to stay alone and required a watchful eye. Jeffrey had only agreed to act as sitter when his stepmother offered to help him buy a car. If she had any idea how little he did in the way of babysitting, she might not have been so generous.

As the girls got closer and closer to their tenth birthdays, they spoke of little else but the initiation ceremony. Eliza, of course, was terrified, and wished she could somehow turn back time, postponing the inevitable.

"You could just tell your mother you don't want to join the sisterhood." Celeste reasoned, knowing even as she said the words that it was impossible.

"No way! The very daughter of the High Priestess! Can you imagine what people would say? She would rather die than be humiliated like that."

"I'm sure it's not as bad as you think. You were a little kid when Anais was sworn in."

"Maybe, but I still remember my sister's screams and in case you forgot, she killed Little Boy Blue."

Even Celeste remembered how long Eliza mourned the death of her beloved pet. The added pain of having to pretend its replacement was the original only fueled her anger and resentment. While all their friends were riding their bikes and sipping soda at the local snack shack, Celeste had sat faithfully by, stroking her hair and wiping away her tears. Finally, when Eliza's pain had turned to anger, she distracted her with sleepovers and tea parties. When Eliza realized her friend didn't share her interest in retribution and was growing tired of listening to her constant replay of events, she simply moved forward on her own.

Prior to joining the coven, Helena insisted that candidates familiarize themselves with the culture and her own children were no exception. Her position within the coven demanded little of her time, as those under her direction did the bulk of the grunt work. The women Helena had chosen to represent the five stations of the pentacle had been a part of her inner circle for more than a decade. The fact that each woman also played an important role in the community itself was no coincidence.

Helena used every tool at her disposal in order to assure the success of the group. Amongst the members were teachers, bankers, shopkeepers, spouses of the local town counsel, as well as descendents of the town's original settlers. They were beyond reproach and while there were still a handful of recent transplants apprehensive about the intentions of the coven, few were willing to voice their concerns.

On Eliza's ninth birthday Helena presented her with a practical guide to witchcraft, which she insisted she read cover to cover. That one was followed with a book on paganism, then it was an introduction to the principles of witchcraft, a basic spell book and a collection of pictorials for the novice herbalist. Every day after school Helena would sit down with Eliza to quiz her on her latest readings. Most days Eliza simply went through the motions, biding her time until the lessons were over, but occasionally she attempted a protest.

"What if I don't want to be in the sister-hood? What if I'd rather study music or join a sport?"

Helena laughed. "The Lewis women don't play sports, Eliza. We have a duty, a responsibility to continue what our ancestor's started and died for. You should be proud of your heritage."

Eliza lowered her head, realizing there was no use in fighting it. Her mother was much too committed to the coven to see things from her own perspective. If her mother had any idea what she intended on doing with the knowledge she was gaining, she might not be so eager for her to learn.

"Stop your pouting Eliza. We still have a lot of work to do. Honestly, I don't understand why you can't be more like your sister. She couldn't wait to be sworn into the coven."

Eliza wanted to puke. She was so tired of being compared to her sister. Not only was Anais more beautiful than Eliza with her silky raven-colored hair and flawless porcelain skin, she also excelled in nearly every venture she undertook, witchcraft being no exception.

Eliza made a mental note to include Anais in whatever sinister plan she ultimately came up with to avenge the unnecessary brutality inflected on her helpless pet.

"Have you decided who you would like to sponsor you for initiation into the coven?" Helena asked.

"Who sponsored Anais?"

"I did, but that isn't the normal course of things, Eliza. Each one of the sisters chooses the novice they think most closely represents their own element. As the High Priestess I mentor only the maiden who will actually take my place as High Priestess some day. I have chosen Anais as my successor. As none of the sisters have offered you up as a candidate, it falls upon me to do so as your mother and leader of the coven, however, you must choose your sponsor."

If she was even slightly interested in joining the coven, Eliza might have been hurt by the fact

that none of her mother's friends had thought her
worthy of initiation into the coven, but it only
made her more determined than ever.

"What about Anais?"

"I'm afraid she is far too busy with her
studies to take on any more responsibilities. How
about Mrs. Putnam?"

Eliza shrugged her shoulders. She could care
less who sponsored her; she had no intention of
playing second fiddle to her mother.

"For the life of me I can't figure you out,
Eliza. Our ancestors paved the way for covens like
ours. They were subjected to hangings, drowning
and much worse for the right to practice witchcraft. This is our heritage. Our people stood all
together against those that sought to bring us
down. Several members of this coven are direct
descendents of some of the most notorious and
powerful witches in history. We have a great
responsibility to those that died before us to
continue the tradition."

As Helena spoke, tears rolled down her
cheeks. For a moment, Eliza felt compelled to
reach out and wrap her arms around her mother,
but she knew only too well the gesture would not
be well received. Instead she lowered her head in
shame, confused by her feelings of both love and
hate for the woman that gave her life. Long ago,
Eliza had learned to choose her words and actions
carefully. She often wished her mother were more

like Celeste's. Her friend's mother was the nicest grown-up she knew. Celeste adored her mother and cherished the time they spent together. Whenever Eliza spent the night at her house, her mother would make sure the girls had everything they could possibly want or need before she went to the coven meetings. When she returned she would sit on the floor with them, telling them stories about princesses in faraway lands while braiding their hair. Afterwards, she would tuck them into bed, leaving the bedroom door slightly ajar so the warmth of the hallway light would cast a welcome comforting glow into the room. Eliza had often wondered if she knew how different things were in her house and if so why she didn't try to stop it.

"Mrs. Putnam will be fine." Eliza muttered. "Should I ask her?"

Helena seemed lost in her own thoughts and Eliza was about to repeat the question when she stood up, indicating their lesson was over.

"I'll take care of it. Run along…you have chores to do."

Eliza wasted no time in retreating to the kitchen where she gathered the trash bag from the kitchen basket and brought it outside. As she dragged the last can to the end of the driveway for the next day's pickup, she could feel her mother's eyes watching her from her bedroom window. When she looked up to confirm the feeling, she saw the curtain quickly fall back into place and her mother's shadowy figure disappear deeper into the room. If she didn't know better, she would think she too had ulterior motives, but Eliza knew she thought far too little of her to expend any energy plotting against her.

With her chores completed, Eliza returned to her room where she quietly locked the door before retrieving the sacred book from behind her bureau. If her mother had noticed its absence, she hadn't mentioned it. Listening intently with her ear to the door to make certain no one was coming before retreating to the furthest corner of her room, Eliza carefully opened the book to the page she had marked the previous day.

Whether her powers were growing stronger or the spells were simply easier to cast, she wasn't certain, but she was becoming more and more confident with each successful outcome. Of course a more mature novice would realize it was just a matter of interpretation as well as the power of belief, but Eliza was convinced that she was the chosen one. Up until now she had focused her training on spiritual spells, but she felt confident enough now to attempt her first personal attack and had chosen her sister Anais as the recipient of her magic.

Running her finger through the index of options, Eliza chose a spell she hoped would make her beautiful sister far less attractive.

According to the book she was required to assemble a concoction of common household products, which combined and applied to the skin would cause her to break out in a horrible rash. Eliza could barely contain her excitement as she went about collecting all of the ingredients before locking herself in the bathroom she shared with her sister. With a steady hand she squeezed the remaining contents from a bottle of facial cream before replacing it with her own mixture. She had barely completed the task when her sister knocked on the door.

"Eliza...are you almost done in there? I need to take a shower."

"Just a minute." Eliza called out, shoving the unused household cleansers under the sink.

Flushing the toilet for good measure, she turned and unlocked the door, barely getting out of Anais' way before she brushed past her. Eliza was about to say something when her sister slammed the door in her face. Normally she would have run to tell her mother, but today she was satisfied her own brand of punishment would be far worse than whatever lame reprimand her mother might hand down. She had only to wait until the following morning when Anais stumbled into the bathroom to relieve herself and get ready for school. Eliza was practically squirming with anticipation while she anxiously awaited her sister's predictable self-admiration in the bathroom's large mirror. She had no sooner flushed the toilet than a piercing scream told Eliza her spell was a success. It was all she could do not to roll over in a fit of laughter.

Helena burst from her room making a bee-line for the girl's bathroom. Feigning concern, Eliza followed at her heels.

"What is it? Anais, are you okay?" Eliza yelled over her sister's hysterical cries.

"My face...look at my face!" Anais cried.

Helena examined her bright-red face which was covered in welts before turning to Eliza.

"What have you done?" She spat.

"I didn't..."

"Don't lie to me. This is obviously the result of an intentional sabotage. You know very well your sister has a formal to attend tomorrow night."

Eliza dropped her head. She had forgotten all about the spring formal. Even she wasn't that cruel. Her sister was a shoe-in for the crown.

"I'm sorry Anais...it was just a joke. I didn't mean..."

Before she could finish the sentence, Anais ran from the room in tears, leaving Eliza alone with her mother to face whatever consequences would come as a result of her cruelty. Eliza braced herself for what was certain to be the harshest punishment her mother could think of, but Helena simply shook her head in disappointment and left the room to comfort her sister. That act alone stung worse than any punishment, physical or otherwise she might have received.

While Eliza endured a day of guilt and school, Anais spent the day with her mother at a health spa in Kennebunkport, where she received a number of facial treatments. When they finally returned home, well after dinner, Anais looked more beautiful than she ever had. Her previously bright red face was now a lovely shade of peach, giving her color where there normally was none. The welts had completely disappeared, replaced with a radiant glow that emphasized her beautiful blue eyes.

Although Eliza attempted to apologize once more, neither Anais nor her mother seemed to be interested in anything she had to say. For the next few days Eliza was treated like a ghost amongst the living. Not only did they exclude her from conversations, but also they absolutely refused to acknowledge her very presence, going so far as to pretend they couldn't see or hear her. Finally, when Eliza had all but given up hope of returning to the fold, both Anais and her mother resumed speaking to her as though nothing had happened.

While life appeared to have returned to normal, Helena began to wonder if perhaps her favoritism toward her eldest daughter might have stoked a fire within Eliza that might not have burned so brightly had she treated them as equals. Although it appeared Eliza likely was testing her abilities by way of elementary spells, Helena was worried that her youngest daughter had targeted her own sister as the recipient of such cruel intent.

Her husband had warned Helena against pitting one sister against the other. While Anais' obvious beauty surpassed her sister's, Eliza did possess an internal beauty beyond reproach. Such a fragile nature needed to be handled with delicate hands and he had worried Helena's obsession with the coven left little room for the patience and the attention Eliza required. Helena refused to even consider his criticism, instead burying her head deeper into the practice. Finally he told her he would no longer tolerate her apparent preference of Anais over her younger sister. Within a week's time he was gone, having passed away in his sleep, or at least that's what Helena told everyone.

While there was speculation around the community that she might have poisoned him, only Helena knew the truth. Not even her sister-hood was privy to what truly went on in the Lewis home and Helena planned on keeping it that way.

Now, however, she was forced to consider whether her husband might have been right and although it pained her, she would find it necessary to spend countless hours in the girl's company in order to insure this was a one-time incident and not the beginning of something more serious.

With Eliza's initiation into the coven less than a year away, Helena suggested she invite her best friend Celeste over for a study session. While it was unusual for her mother to allow someone other than the sisterhood into their home, Eliza was so excited she didn't give it much thought.

"Perhaps your friend could spend the night. We can order pizza and then bake some cookies." Helena suggested.

Eliza rushed into her mother's arms, hugging her tight.

"I'll call her right away." Eliza called over her shoulder as she ran from the room.

Twenty minutes later, Celeste, along with her mother arrived on the doorstep.

"Are you sure you want her to spend the night?"

"Absolutely. In fact, I'm more than overdue to return the favor. Eliza practically lives at your house."

After a brief chat about coven business, Celeste's mother left them, leaving her nervous daughter in the hands of the High Priestess.

"Why don't you girls run along upstairs with Celeste's bag and I'll gather a few things for our lesson."

The girls had nodded in unison before they disappeared up the stairs in giggles.

Helena retreated to the kitchen where she collected a pink candle, a piece of parchment, oil, quill and ink along with matches and a small bowl. She had just returned to the sitting room and was placing the articles on the floor when the two girls bounded down the stairs.

"Will Anais be joining us?" Eliza asked, hoping her sister had other plans.

"No, it will just be the three of us tonight. Your sister is spending the night at a friend's house."

Eliza attempted to feign disappointment but it was obvious even to Celeste she was excited to have her mother all to herself and her best friend.

"What spell are we going to do?" She asked excitedly.

"I thought it would be nice to do a friendship spell. Now, just watch carefully so you can perform it on your own one day."

Helena took the pink votive candle in one hand while dipping her fingers from the other into a small bowl of oil. Next she rubbed the oil onto the candle in a downward motion from the top to the middle and then upward from the bottom to the middle before placing it directly onto the floor.

"Now you should each write your name on the parchment and then fold it in half."

The girls took turns writing their names, each struggling with the awkward quill before Eliza folded the paper in half and handed it back to her mother.

"Now there really are no official words to be spoken, each sister must use her own words to cast her spell. For the purpose of teaching you, I will take lead tonight."

Placing the folded paper on the floor, Helena struck a match, lighting the pink candle before retrieving it.

"In the name of our sacred sisterhood I ask the Goddess bless the friendship between Eliza and Celeste that they may forever be bound in peace and friendship."

Helena placed the parchment against the flame, igniting the fragile paper and sending ashes raining down to the floor. Eliza and Celeste watched wide-eyed as the paper disappeared, leaving only the fragrant candle burning brightly in its wake.

"Do we blow out the candle now?" Celeste whispered.

"No, the candle must burn completely for the spell to work. You must continue to meditate, concentrating on your love for each other."

The candle burned quickly with the added fuel from the oil and just when Eliza and Celeste were beginning to feel the pain of pins and needles from sitting in one position for too long, the flame finally went out, leaving a puddle of hot wax and ashes in its place.

"Now, girls, you should never do a candle spell without an adult present. The flame could easily get out of hand. Our magic is very powerful and if we aren't careful we can cause great harm. Our coven has no room for dark or hurtful magic, only the purest of candidates can join our ranks."

"But what if someone tries to hurt us?" Eliza asked cautiously.

"We don't use our powers for individual gain, Eliza. Only when it benefits the sisterhood as a whole do we consider action and even then we use discretion. Now why don't you two clean this up while I order us a pizza, okay?"

"Okay." The girls agreed in unison.

After pizza and cookies, Helena tuned the old black and white television to a classic horror movie, confident the girls would fall asleep well before it ended. The old television had been a wedding gift from her in-laws and had been a prized possession of her husband's. Although it still worked fine, the girls continually begged for a color TV like everyone they knew had. While even Helena agreed that it would be nice to own a newer model, she simply couldn't afford one at the moment. Living off the sale of homegrown herbs as well as the little cash she received from reading palms, she was barely squeaking by.

Perhaps when the girls got a little older she might consider opening up a shop in town, but for now she was forced to live within her meager means, even if that meant going without some of the luxuries most other people would consider necessities.

As expected, the girls feel asleep on the sofa halfway through the movie and Helena covered them with a blanket before turning off the lights and making her way up to her bedroom where she changed into her nightclothes and gathered her notebook to begin her plan for the next meeting of the coven.

Chapter Two

The months dragged by slowly as both Eliza and Celeste waited for their initiation into the coven. While Eliza continued to have mixed feelings, Celeste eagerly counted down the days on a special moon phase calendar her mother had given her. Perhaps it was the different methods of teachings each girl received through their sponsors that made their interpretations of the material so contradictory, but whatever it was, Celeste found herself questioning her friendship with Eliza more and more.

"Who cares if the moon is full or not? We can still do the spell." Eliza insisted.

"It won't work unless the elements are aligned and you know it." Celeste retorted.

"It's just a stupid spell anyway. Never mind, I'll do it by myself."

Eliza stormed off leaving Celeste alone in the old shack behind her grandmother's house. As for Eliza, she ran home as fast as she could, hoping to tell her side of the story before Celeste's mother gave hers an earful. Unfortunately she wasn't fast enough and as she ran up the porch steps her mother was waiting for her at the door with a grim look on her face.

"Would you like to explain why you left Celeste in tears at her grandmother's house?" Helena questioned, dragging Eliza through the entry by her ponytail.

"She's just being a baby. I just wanted to do a stupid spell and she refused to help me."

Helena planted her daughter on the bottom step of the staircase, forcing Eliza to look up in fear.

"First of all, young lady, there are rules about performing magic without your sponsor being present. Let's not forget, you haven't been sworn into the coven yet and at this rate, may never be. Secondly and more importantly, magic should never come between you and your friendship with Celeste."

Eliza lowered her eyes, ashamed not only for being caught, but for hurting her best friend.

"I'm not interested in knowing what spell you were attempting, nor am I interested in whatever lie you are concocting in that little brain of yours to explain why you disobeyed the basic rules of conduct the coven has set forth. What I will hear is an apology, not only to Celeste, but to your sponsor, to whom you have brought shame. After that you can consider yourself no longer a candidate for our coven."

"But Mother, please...I'm sorry. It won't happen again." Eliza cried.

"You're right, it will not happen again, because from this moment forward, you are banned from practicing magic. Gather all your books and return them to me."

Eliza remained seated, staring at her mother in shock.

"Now, Eliza...don't make me ask twice."

Eliza burst into tears, "It's not fair. I said I was sorry."

Helena merely turned her back and walked away, leaving her daughter sobbing. Helena hoped the pain of losing a spot in the coven would scare her enough to take things a little more seriously. She would let her stew it over for a week or so to let it really sink in before she invited her back into the coven. Her role as the High Priestess gave her the power to confirm or reject a candidate and she intended to teach her daughter a valuable lesson.

Eliza pulled herself up off the step and made the long climb up to her room to retrieve her books. As she passed by Anais she avoided making eye contact, knowing her sister would use the opportunity to make her feel even worse than she already did. Instead she made a beeline for her bureau, keeping her head down and quickly gathering her books and notebooks before returning downstairs. She could hear her mother talking softly on the phone and heard her name mentioned more than once but otherwise was unable to make out the conversation. Rather than risk being caught eavesdropping, she made her way back upstairs and locked herself in her bedroom.

It seemed that every time a storm passed another more powerful eruption came in its wake. As if the elements were somehow linked to her mood, the skies opened up and it began to pour. The heavy rain and winds brought back painful memories from the past. Alone once more without the comfort of her mother or sister, the feelings of betrayal she had recently set aside came back with a vengeance. Helena had made it a point to spend one night a week with Eliza and even occasionally Celeste, teaching them the ways of the coven. The time she spent with her mother had made her feel special and she regretted wasting so many years plotting against her. Even Anais had made an attempt, although probably under duress.

As the storm intensified, so too did Eliza's hurt and anger. How could her mother be so cruel? How could she ever leave her house again without feeling the eyes of the entire community upon her? Celeste would probably never speak to her again, especially if she was banned from the coven as well. It seemed unlikely but perhaps she could put in a good word for Celeste if it wasn't too late. After all, Celeste had refused to do the spell and that had to count for something. Wiping her tears away, Eliza rolled off the bed and made her way downstairs, finding her mother tending her herb garden.

"Mother?"

"What is it, Eliza?"

Eliza took a deep breath to steady her nerves. "Celeste won't be banned from the coven will she? It was my idea to do the spell and she refused to do it."

"That's up to Celeste's mother. As far as I'm concerned, she is still welcome to join."

Eliza was about to ask if her mother might reconsider her ban, but she didn't want to push her luck. Returning to the solitude of her room, she considered her options. Whether her mother would allow it or not, she had no intention of giving up magic.

For the next several days Celeste used every excuse she could come up with to avoid spending time alone with Eliza. Her mother was taking the matter under consideration and hadn't yet decided whether or not she would be allowed to become a member of the coven. Until she knew for sure, she wasn't about to risk being seen alone with her friend. She could see the pain in Eliza's eyes and she wanted nothing more than to tell her how very sorry she was for telling her grandmother and getting her in trouble. Ultimately though, it didn't make a difference. Celeste too was banned from joining the coven, perhaps merely for causing her mother embarrassment.

While Helena had originally planned on removing the ban once Eliza learned her lesson, the subject never came up and she proceeded without her.

If her mother wasn't the High Priestess, the day of the initiation might have passed without Eliza noticing, but so much preparation was involved she couldn't avoid it. With the Summer Solstice drawing near, it was all anyone could talk about, at least those in her inner circle. To add salt to the wound, Helena asked her to gather flowers she would use to make wreaths for the candidates' heads. The phone rang continuously with each member confirming her own contribution to the ceremony. Eliza was enlisted to act as secretary, making notes while Helena weaved the wreaths.

Never once did she consider how Eliza might feel knowing that she wouldn't be allowed to participate.

Even at the tender age of ten, Eliza was old enough to see the difference between what her mother proclaimed to be a coven of good witches and what they truly were. While she acted the part of the High Priestess, manipulating the elements in the name of white magic, she secretly plotted against anyone that might stand in her way of becoming the most powerful witch of her time. All the pomp and circumstance displayed during the monthly gatherings and public spectacles were nothing more than smoke and mirrors to hide her true intentions.

While Eliza dutifully assisted her mother in preparation of the evening's events, her mind was occupied with her own diabolical plan. Although Helena had arranged for Theona, one of the watchers, to stay behind with her daughter in case she had any notion to sneak off, Eliza had already snuck into her mother's medicine cabinet where she stole a couple of sleeping pills. Once she had rendered the watcher unconscious, she would be free to escape unnoticed.

Although the ceremony wouldn't take place until midnight, Helena and Anais left the house early to see to preparations, leaving Eliza with a woman she barely knew.

"You mind Sister Theona and go to bed when she tells you to!" Helena instructed.

Theona placed her arm over Eliza's slim shoulders.

"We'll do just fine. You just enjoy the celebration and don't worry about a thing."

Helena gazed at her daughter causing Eliza to lower her eyes. If she didn't know better she would think her mother knew what she was up to, but she had been extremely careful planning her revenge, taking time to gather what she needed slowly so as not to draw attention. Convinced her daughter was up to something, Helena hesitated.

"Maybe I should call upon another sister to assist you?"

"Don't be silly…everything will be fine."

"Eliza?"

"We'll be fine." She agreed, assuring her mother with a weak smile.

"Alright then. We should be back before two."

Theona and Eliza watched as Helena and Anais loaded the supplies into the back of the old station wagon and backed out of the driveway. When the car drove out of sight, Eliza sprang into action.

"Do you want to play a game of cards?" Eliza asked.

"That's a great idea." Theona agreed.

"They're in the side table drawer. Why don't you get them while I get the cookies my mother made for us?"

Without waiting for a response, Eliza ran into the kitchen and poured a couple glasses of milk. Sneaking the pills she had stolen out of her pants pocket, she dropped them into one of the glasses before retrieving the plate of cookies and returning to the sitting room.

Eliza anxiously watched for over an hour, as Theona grew more and more groggy. Twice she briefly nodded off, only to wake up again.

"My goodness, it must be getting late. Why don't you run up and brush your teeth and go to bed. If you'd like I can come up and tuck you in."

"I'm ten, I don't need to be tucked in." Eliza insisted.

"Okay then." Theona yawned, grateful she didn't have to attempt the stairs in her current condition. "Goodnight."

"Goodnight."

Eliza climbed the stairs slowly, listening for any sound of movement from below. After a brief clinking sound which she assumed was Theona straightening up the coffee table, she heard her kick her shoes off and lie down on the sofa.

Positioning herself on the top step, she sat patiently and waited until sounds of light snoring drifted up to the second floor.

This was the moment she had been waiting for and her entire body tingled with excitement. Rushing up to the attic that had frightened her so badly she had nightmares for nearly a year, she ran up the steps and retrieved the disgusting fisher spider she had plucked out of the Little Ell Pond a few days before. No spell could come close to the effect the hairy creature would have on her sister, who feared nothing worse. Trapped inside an old goldfish bowl with a sheet of plastic wrap covering the opening, the spider skimmed the surface of the murky water she had collected at the same time. Slowly she made her way back down the steps, stopping briefly to listen for any movement down below before heading to her sister's bureau, where she proceeded to nudge the spider with the aid of a comb onto a nightgown she was certain to look for when she came home.

After draining the contents of the bowl into the bathroom sink and returning it to the attic, Eliza snuck downstairs and seized a box of rat poisoning from beneath the kitchen sink, which she proceeded to blend into her mother's sugar bowl, confident she would never taste it in her morning coffee. Pleased her actions would serve their purpose without either her mother or her sister knowing her involvement, she climbed the stairs, brushed her teeth and went to bed.

It wasn't over. She was just getting started. If Helena had taught her anything it was patience. If Eliza could wait ten years to join the coven only to be denied entry weeks before her initiation, she could wait just a little longer to settle the score. Besides, she rather liked the idea of prolonging their misery. What better way to spend a summer than sit back and watch her mother's agonizing slow death. Once she was out of the way, Anais would no longer be a problem.

While Eliza drifted off to sleep, Helena and her coven of sisters had completed their performance at the Annual Town Hall Celebration. The celebration had become bigger than anyone could have imagined. What began as a small festival for the locals to kick off the summer had turned into a huge tourist event. People came from all over New England and beyond to take part in the now famous walking tour of the town's historical sites, followed by a gathering at the Town Hall and a bonfire on the beach. Helena used the distraction to her advantage, performing their private ritual out in the open with no one the wiser.

Because the town's history was rich with connections to the Salem Witch Trials, the town council always invited the coven to perform a candlelight ceremony at the town hall. The more outrageous it was, the more attention they received and tourists flocked in by the busloads. While the town stuffed its pockets, they turned a blind eye to anything questionable involving the coven. While the beach itself – along with the quaint shops and restaurants – brought in enough business on their own, the occult element set them apart from other destinations that might offer the same.

With the bonfire well underway, Helena and the rest of the coven made their way to a secluded spot on the beach in order to perform the initiation ceremony. With only the distant, dim light of the bonfire and the glow of the full moon, the candidates were brought forward one at a time.

"Who comes to this sacred place?"

"I am Kimberly, spawn of the earth and heavens."

"Who speaks for you?"

"It is I, Ember, who vouches for her."

"You are entering a place of power, a place beyond imagining. As you step between the worlds, you stand on the threshold of the eternal life. Are you strong enough?"

"I am."

"Then prepare for your rebirth."

Kimberly and her sponsor stepped aside as the next two candidates were presented.

When all three girls had committed themselves, their sponsors then stepped forward and removed their robes, exposing their naked bodies. As the sponsors covered their candidate's eyes with blindfolds, the remaining members of the coven stepped forward to assist in the bathing ritual, cleansing them of their previous lives. Once dry, the girls were draped in white robes to signify their purity.

Stepping out of the darkness clad in a long black robe, Helena approached the candidates.

"Have you all come to us of your own free will?"

"We have." The girls responded in unison.

"Are you willing to suffer to prove your commitment?"

"We are."

Helena waited as the challenger presented her with a blade. Accepting the instrument, she took the right hand of each girl and pressed the blade into the heel of each of their hands to extract a small amount of blood before pressing it against her heart.

"Repeat after me... I solemnly swear to protect and defend my sisters of the coven. I vow to never reveal any secrets of the coven. I swear on my mother's womb and my eternal life, and in the presence of those before me."

With the help of their sponsors each girl rose.

"Come and be anointed."

Helena dipped her fingers into a vessel of oil and anointed the forehead of each of the girls with the sign of the pentagram.

"You have all been accepted into the coven. You may each choose a name to represent your element by which you will be addressed in the future."

With that the remaining members of the coven formed a circle around the three girls, welcoming them into their fold.

It was nearly three in the morning when Helena and Anais finally returned home. Telling her daughter to run along upstairs and go to bed, Helena made her way into the sitting room where she found Theona snoring softly. Normally she might have woken her and sent her on her way, but she was so exhausted herself, she merely tiptoed out of the room and up the stairs.

She had just finished changing into her nightclothes and was about to brush her teeth when Anais let out a piercing shriek. Dropping her toothbrush into the sink, she ran for her daughter's room where she found her trembling in a heap on the floor.

"What is it? You scared me half to death."

"There's a huge spider in my drawer."

"Oh, for God's sake, Anais! Get a grip."

Angry at her eldest daughter's overreaction, Helena stomped over to the open drawer and peered inside. Spotting the spider crawling into the neck of a nightgown, she tossed the garment onto the floor and drove her heel down into the fabric.

"Was that so difficult? Honestly." Without a soothing word to comfort her hysterical child, Helena turned and walked out the door.

For Anais there would be no sleep that night, only vivid nightmares of hairy eight-legged monsters. Her sister however, smiled and rolled over; pleased things were finally turning in her favor.

Chapter Three

The summer was just beginning and Eliza was anxious to get out of the stuffy old house and spread her wings. The house reeked of sickness as Helena continued to struggle to keep anything down. It had been nearly a week since Eliza had laced the sugar bowl with rat poison and despite her mother's decision to switch from coffee to herbal tea to settle her stomach, she continued to sweeten it with the tainted sugar. Just in case she grew suspicious, Eliza pretended to be feeling a little under the weather herself for a day or two. The act paid off and Helena was convinced there was a stomach bug going around. Thinking she had suffered long enough, Eliza dumped the remaining sugar from the bowl, washed it and refilled it without the additional ingredient.

Although her relationship with Celeste wasn't quite back to normal, her friend invited her to spend a few days at the beach with her grand-parents. A distraction was just what she needed to clear her head. It was sad really that a ten-year-old should be so burdened and obsessed with such sinister matters. While most children her young age rarely thought about their future, or much be-yond the present day for that matter, she spent nearly every waking moment planning her next move. For the past week she had done nothing but read from the book of shadows, hoping to find a spell worthy of her dark mood.

She had come to realize Anais was as much a victim of their mother's cruelty as she was and she actually felt bad about hiding the spider in her sister's room. While she didn't plan on the two of them becoming friends any time soon, she felt they could coexist in the same house without too much effort.

Her mother, however, was another matter and Eliza wouldn't stop until she put her in her grave. The older she got, the more she became convinced of her mother's involvement in her father's death. As far as Eliza was concerned, she deserved the same. While she packed her bag, she considered her options once more. There was a spell that caused hallucinations as well as one that promised temporary paralysis. The latter required the venom of a cottonmouth snake, which would be impossible to come by. The first spell seemed the better option and all she had to do was locate either morning glories or nightshade. The other items required to perform the spell were things she could easily find around the house. Confident in her ability to execute the spell, Eliza only needed to bide her time and wait for the right moment to send her mother over the edge.

Hearing the doorbell chime, she tossed the rest of her clothes into her bag, stopping briefly in the bathroom to retrieve a hairbrush, toothpaste and her toothbrush before bounding down the stairs.

"Are you sure you're feeling up to this? I know you were only sick a couple of days, but if you're not careful it might come back." Helena warned.

"I'm fine really...besides, aren't you always saying fresh air is the best medicine?"

"That's true...okay but if you change your mind and want to come home just have Celeste's grandmother give me a call."

Eliza nodded, pausing briefly in case her mother wanted to hug her goodbye, but she merely turned and headed back into the kitchen. The doorbell chimed again and Eliza realized her mother had never bothered to open the door.

Alone in the house, Helena was finally starting to feel better. Although she was far from being her normal healthy self, she at least had the energy to do a little light cleaning. For the past few weeks she had done the bare minimum in regards to housework and evidence of her neglect was all around her.

Helena was the fourth generation to have claimed ownership to the old home and if she didn't figure something out soon it wouldn't stand long enough to see a fifth. The exterior hadn't seen a coat of paint in nearly two decades, thanks in part to her lazy husband. The white paint fell from the structure like snow during a blizzard, blanketing the overgrown shrubs and neglected perennials whenever the wind blew. What once stood as a testament to the family's wealth and power now merely reflected their isolation from anyone not connected to the sisterhood. The home's many windows, previously sandwiched between brown shutters, exposed decades old draperies behind dirty glass. While many of the wooden shutters had rotted away, others hung askew; their hardware long ago released from the unprotected wood. The formerly striking wrap-around porch had lost its luster years ago and had turned into a safety hazard with missing floor-boards and loose steps. The grounds themselves were overrun with weeds and grass high enough to reach her knees. While Helena made it a point to continually complain about the condition of her home in hopes that someone might take pity on her, no one took the bait. Instead her friends had suggested local landscapers and handymen that they had used in the past. Her hopes that one of them might offer up the services of their husband or brothers were shattered. With their suspicions regarding her own husband, not even her closest friends were willing to lend out their loved ones for fear they might not return.

The interior, although not as dilapidated as the outside, was dated and showing its age from years of neglect. The walls of the main floor of the house were covered in Victorian Era wallpaper, long ago faded. The heavy paper with its faded colors made the rooms feel small and dark. The wall sconces in the hallway required candles and therefore were of no use at all other than to collect dust and cobwebs. The woodwork surrounding the windows and doorways as well as the crown molding and staircase was ornate and typical of the period the house was built in and would have been stunning in its day, but it was well overdue for a proper cleaning and polishing. Although there were hardwood floors throughout the home, they too were in need of stripping and staining to bring back their original shine. Had she the means, she might have hired a housekeeper or handyman to tend to such things, but she was barely making ends meet as it was and such frivolous spending was simply out of the question. Her mother had seen to the renovation of the home's kitchen and bathrooms in the early '50s and while they were definitely dated, they were fully functional and therefore of little concern. Other than the formal sitting room and a few of the bedroom pieces belonging to her great-grandparents, her parents purchased most of the furnishings before she was born. Looking around the room, Helena realized, perhaps for the first time, that very little of the décor was of her own choosing.

While Helena had always kept a clean house, she had never appreciated it for its true beauty. Having lived there all her life, she neither liked nor disliked the home. As a child she was constantly reminded of the family's villainous past, or at least what others presumed to be evil. The original home, built by the Lewis family back in the late 1600s, had been burned to the ground shortly after the Salem Witch Trials.

After a series of unfortunate accidents involving several unexplained deaths on the Lewis property, it was impossible to locate any laborers willing to step foot on the grounds. It took nearly all the family's fortune and three generations of descendants to build the home that still stood witness to a practice few understood and many feared.

Unlike Eliza, who seemed either unable or unwilling to comprehend the magnitude of her ancestor's sacrifices, Helena's understanding was taught through example. Her own mother had tied her to a stake and threatened to set her on fire. She had been used like a pincushion for sacrificial blood, hung upside down while her fellow sisters took turns slicing into her flesh just for the mere spectacle of it all. Years before her own initiation into the coven, she had also been forced to digest various concoctions in the name of research. Her own mother was well known for her skills as an herbalist as well as a botanist. If the patrons of her goods had known she used her daughter as a test subject, none of them seemed to care. As long as her brews worked, that was all that mattered to them. Helena shuttered at the memories of her past. For all her effort to put the past behind her, the memories continued to haunt her.

With Eliza off with Celeste's family and Anais out doing whatever it was girls her age were doing, Helena had the place all to herself. It was a luxury she rarely knew and after considering the enormity of the work that lay ahead of her as well as her weakened state, she decided it couldn't hurt to indulge in a little herbal cocktail of her own.

After locking the front door to make sure she wasn't interrupted, she made her way to a small wooden box lying atop the fireplace mantel. Placing the box on the coffee table, she peered out the window one more time before lifting the cover and removing the inner compartment that held a small sewing kit. She smiled, thinking, *what a perfect place it was to hide my stash.*

Not only did she rarely sew other than to darn a sock or secure a button, neither of the girls had shown any interest in learning the skill.

Under the compartment was a satin bag that contained rolling paper, a lighter and a small amount of marijuana, which she withdrew; then quickly setting to work on rolling a cigarette. By the time Anais returned home, Helena didn't have a care in the world.

Chapter Four

With Helena preparing for the Harvest Moon and Anais otherwise occupied with the son of a local restaurateur, Eliza had continued her research unnoticed. Very little had changed over the summer to detour her from her mission, despite the fact she appeared to be on her own. Celeste spent the summer bouncing back and forth between Wells and Kennebunkport, leaving little time for Eliza. When school finally resumed in September, however, the two picked up where they left off as if no time had passed at all. Celeste found middle school difficult to adjust to. Her friendship with Eliza seemed to place her under a social microscope she was ill prepared for. While Eliza appeared not to notice, the intense scrutiny of her classmates, it nearly crippled Celeste. Like most young girls, their classmates were nothing if not curious and more than willing to risk it all to get a glimpse into the mystical realm.

Being virtually invisible, at least through her mother's eyes, Eliza had just enough freedom to come and go as she pleased with little or no fuss. By the end of September she had secured enough influence with her peers to form her own coven. Although Celeste continued to protest, fearful their parents would find out, Eliza solidified the newfound assembly with a blood oath and a vow of secrecy.

"Any member who tells will be cast from the coven and cursed for the rest of her life." She warned.

While Celeste took the threat with a grain of salt, the other members only nodded, fearing her wrath. By Halloween Eliza had convinced nearly all the girls she was not to be messed with. Not only had she sacrificed a frog to frighten a teacher who dared to give her a failing grade on a quiz, but when a sixth grader provoked her by inviting the boy she liked to the Autumn Ball, she laced her hair brush with superglue causing the poor girl to rip out a large section of hair by the roots.

Horrified by the lengths she would go to in order to get her way, the obedient members jumped at her every command. All that was except for Celeste.

Donning a headscarf to cover her bald spot, the latest victim of Eliza's wrath, made her way through the crowded hallways of the middle school with her eyes on the floor.

"Serves her right." Eliza spat.

"It's a little cruel if you ask me." Celeste mumbled under her breath.

"Don't be such a baby. She knew I liked Timmy and she asked him out anyway."

"So why didn't you ask him first?" Celeste challenged.

Eliza glared at her friend, searching for the appropriate response.

"He should have asked me. It doesn't matter anyway because there's no way he's going to take her now. I'll give him a day or two to ask me and if he doesn't we'll do a love spell."

Celeste simply rolled her eyes, knowing it was useless to argue with her friend. She had known her long enough to recognize when her mind was made up. It didn't matter if she was right or wrong or whether or not anyone agreed, as long as she got what she wanted in the end. As they walked to their next class in silence, Celeste considered whether or not she should simply break ties with Eliza all together.

If it wasn't for the fact her mother served under Helena, she might have done so back when she was banned from the sisterhood. On more than one occasion she had overheard her own mother complain about the direction the High Priestess seemed to be moving, wondering if perhaps she was dabbling in black magic. For reasons beyond her understanding, her mother was continuing her allegiance in spite of her fears and reservations.

The following day after school, Eliza called for a gathering to take place in the woods surrounding their old elementary school. As the group moved through a thicket of prickly bushes, the audible complaints of her sisters made their way to Eliza's ears. Stopping abruptly, she spun around to face the protestors.

"If you can't deal with a few scratches, how do you expect to survive the challenge?"

"What challenge?" Celeste asked on behalf of her suddenly mute companions.

"I decided we should challenge the bravery of our sisters to make sure they are worthy of their positions."

Celeste shook her head. "You can't just make stuff up like that. There has to be a vote."

"I'm the High Priestess so I can do whatever I want. Of course, if they're too scared they can always leave the coven."

All eyes dropped to the ground, avoiding contact with their leader. Celeste shook her head once more, angry that the girls refused to stand up to Eliza. Amused by their fear, Eliza turned and continued to walk deeper into the woods. When they finally arrived at a small clearing used by the local teenagers as a drinking spot, she motioned for the girls to sit. A number of toppled trees had been dragged across the ground to form a circle around a fire pit for use as seating.

"How did you find this place?" Misty asked; frightened yet intrigued by her surroundings.

"I followed my sister one night when she snuck out of the house. I figured if she didn't have my mom's permission she must be up to something bad." Eliza snickered, happy to finally divulge the secret.

Celeste raised her eyebrows. "I can't believe she'd risk getting caught."

"Well, she did and she didn't. Get caught, that is. It was stupid, though. But when she got here there were already a bunch of kids smoking cigarettes and drinking beer."

Now she had the attention of all the girls who wanted to know the details. Did they know any of the older kids? Was everyone making out? Why didn't she stay and see what happened? Eliza soaked in the attention, embellishing whenever necessary while leaving out the actual fear and excitement she felt as she watched the teenagers. She might have stayed longer had a couple of the boys not headed in her direction to relieve themselves, she told them.

"Did you tell Anais that you had followed her?" Celeste asked, curious why this was the first she was hearing about the incident.

"No way. She would have found a way to tell my mother without making herself look bad and then I'd never be able to sneak out again."

The girls nodded in unison, having siblings of their own. When everyone finally settled down, Eliza stood and addressed the group.

"Okay, so I was thinking it's time to start testing our skills so I've come up with a list of spells for each of you to try. I'll read the list and then you can each pick the spell that you're most comfortable with."

The girls nodded in compliance.

One by one Eliza listed the spells, pausing in between to gauge the groups reaction.

"Number one...summon a familiar, number two...cast a love spell, number three...a dream spell..."

After completing the list Eliza sat down to wait for the group to make their decisions. The weakest members of the group choose quickly opting for spells there was no way of knowing whether or not it had worked, thereby avoiding embarrassment or chastising from their leader. However, a few others, including Celeste, lingered in thought.

Finally Eliza's patience wore out. "For Pete's sake, Celeste, just make a decision. You're supposed to be my maiden."

Celeste bit her tongue fighting the urge to tell her she never asked to be the second in command.

"Fine…the love spell."

"Perfect, I was hoping you'd choose that one." Eliza passed one of the remaining index cards to her friend, which included the ingredients necessary to perform the spell as well as detailed instructions.

Celeste scanned the card and turned ghastly white before quickly rising and tossing the card back in Eliza's lap.

"What's wrong with you? I don't want anything to do with you or your coven ever again." With that she burst into tears and ran back in the direction they had came, leaving the group shocked and confused by what had just happened. Not to be upstaged by the outburst, Eliza rolled over in a fit of laughter as the girls tried to figure out what they had missed. Finally, when attention was back on her, Eliza explained.

"I guess Celeste just isn't brave enough to handle a little period blood. I guess I'll have to take this one myself."

Still confused, but too afraid to voice their ignorance, the remaining members of the coven set to work strategizing how they might come about the various objects required to cast their spells.

While she put on a confident front, inside Eliza worried she might have not only lost her best friend but also gained an opponent that she wasn't prepared to do battle with. If Celeste was upset enough, she might tell her mother what Eliza was up to and she would most certainly tell the High Priestess. After the incident that left them both out of her mother's coven, Celeste had promised to never tell on her again, but that was a long time ago and they had never discussed it again. If her mother found out about her coven she would be furious. The thought of having to disband what she had worked so hard to put together both frightened and infuriated her at the same time. She would be the laughing stock of the school.

All Celeste had to do was tell one person, the queen herself; the leader of the cheering squad, and that's exactly what she did. The following day the school was buzzing with gossip and Eliza was left to suffer the embarrassment alone.

Chapter Five

While Eliza's secret coven marched forward
without incident, she spent the next several
months focusing her newly found confidence on
perfecting one spell in particular. Whether it was
due to the fact she was now alone since Celeste
was out of the picture or because her mother's
indifference toward her only fueled her hatred, she
wasn't certain. Whatever the reason, she was more
determined than ever to see her suffer. She had
finally located the elusive nightshade amongst her
mother's pharmacy of herbal concoctions after
months of searching the roadsides and overgrown
fields abutting the property. If the plant grew
anywhere in Wells it would be in her own back
yard, where generations of Lewis women had
produced their personal supply of revenge. She
spent countless hours roaming the fields with no
success and was on the verge of calling it quits

when she discovered a secret stash of plants strung up to dry on a clothes line behind her father's old tool shed.

The accidental discovery convinced the novice she was embarking on a path approved by a higher power. Perhaps her father's spirit had led her there. After all, the shed was where he spent most of his days. Even though she was too young to understand the nature of their arguments, the sound of loud slamming doors still haunted her memories. However it started, it always ended the same. Her mother would scream at him to get out and point to the door. Her father would march across the room, fling open the door and slam it behind him. Next, her mother would tell her and her sister to go to their room as if it were some-how their fault and she would watch her father from her bedroom window as he made the long walk across the overgrown field to his tool shed. Before he entered the shed he would always look back up the hill as if he was searching for some-one. Eliza would always wave, hoping her father would be comforted by her acknowledgement. Now, looking up that same hill she realized it was highly unlikely he could see her tiny frame at such a distance.

Examining the cuttings carefully she found the bunch tagged nightshade and removed several leaves from the sprigs, making sure to take only a couple from each branch. Placing them in the bag she had tucked in her pocket, she made her way to the front of the shed where she pulled back the rusty latch. Her father had never allowed them to enter while he was alive, claiming there were snakes nesting in the rafters. Eliza cautiously opened the door, letting the light filter through before stepping inside. As her eyes began to adjust to the room, she froze with panic, not by what she saw, as she could make out very little, but because of the overwhelming feeling of being watched. As carefully as she'd entered, she retreated, securing the latch and making her way as quickly as she could back across the field.

That evening she went to bed early claiming exhaustion. Helena was too busy fawning over Anais' latest accomplishments to pay her any attention. Only Anais stopped what she was doing to wish her "goodnight" before returning to her work.

Once in her room, Eliza secured the lock on her door before retrieving the family grimoire from behind her bureau. While she thumbed through the thick pages in search of the spell, she listened for any sound which might indicate that someone was coming. With the coast clear, she carefully opened a bag of her mother's favorite jasmine tea, spilling the contents into a small bowl. Next she added the nightshade that she had collected earlier and crushed it into the mixture before adding a droplet of jasmine oil to mask any scent of the deadly plant. Her hands shook as she fumbled with the tea bag, making it difficult to refill. Finally confident there was enough of the combination for its intended purpose, she clasped the tiny staple back in place and then set it on the radiator to dry. Now all she had to do was say the words she had composed months earlier and the spell would be complete.

> "From all the souls of those that passed, this revenge spell I do cast.
> "To my mother I solemnly vow, to make her pay here and now.
> "For all the evil that she has done, including the lies that she has spun.
> "May she suffer day and night, with halluci-nations aimed to fright.
> "Not until she admits her guilt, will I stop this curse I built."

Despite the warmth given off by the hot radiator, a chill ran down her spine causing her to shiver in its wake. Quickly she returned the book to its hiding place and unlocked her door before tucking the remaining items safely under her bed. She had no sooner turned out the light and got into bed than her mother opened the door to check on her. Eliza held her breath, hoping she wouldn't notice the teabag drying on the cast iron radiator, but her worry was for naught as her mother merely peered into the darkness before closing the door and retreating down the hall.

Though exhausted, sleep didn't come easy for Eliza as she tossed and turned throughout the night. Heaviness hung over her, tormenting her with images of her father. Perhaps the entry into his private sanctuary brought back memories she has chosen to repress to protect herself from the pain of his loss. Whatever the reason, she couldn't shake the feeling that she wasn't alone.

Outside the airstream grew in intensity as a pre-winter snowstorm blew into the area, and the single-paned window adjacent to Eliza's bed shook with enough force to dislodge an amulet she kept there for protection, tossing it to the floor.

Bolting upright, the young girl clutched her blankets as her eyes scanned the room. As another gust of wind brought freezing rain that pelted the already fragile window, the now dry teabag slid off the radiator, coming to rest atop the amulet. Eliza's mind raced to interpret the message the elements were attempting to send. Maybe her mother's powers were so great the elements were protecting her from the spell that she had cast or perhaps her father was trying to send her a message that he approved of her plan. Whatever the meaning, Eliza was certain of one thing. Her premonition that she was being watched had now been proven.

It wasn't until the sun began to rise that she finally laid her head to rest, placing the amulet back on the windowsill and tucking the teabag under her pillow for safe keeping. Comforted by the notion that her father was watching over her, she slipped into a dreamless sleep.

An hour later, Anais flung open her door to announce school had been cancelled due to icy conditions.

Eliza grunted her acknowledgment before rolling over and falling back to sleep. By the time she finally rolled out of bed, it was nearly noon. She could hear her mother and sister discussing plans for the winter solstice with great enthusiasm. She half expected them to stop talking as soon as she entered the kitchen, if for no other reason than to spare her the excitement that they felt over a celebration she was unwelcome to attend, but they merely nodded their greetings and continued on as if she wasn't there.

"Can I heat up the teakettle for some hot cocoa?" She interrupted.

Helena briefly looked in her direction, annoyed by the intrusion.

"Fine but be careful not to burn yourself."

Eliza nodded, making her way past the pair with the empty pot to the sink, where she refilled it. While she waited for the water to boil, she listened for a break in their conversation. When it finally came and she made her move.

"Would you like a cup of tea, Mother?"

"Yes, thank you, Eliza. Perhaps your sister would like some hot cocoa as well."

Anais smiled at her younger sister. "That would be lovely, Eliza." She agreed.

Eliza smiled back – no longer envious of her sister's beauty. She had finally come to realize that beauty had just as many drawbacks as it did advantages. Eliza often heard her sister cry over a broken heart, something she was unlikely to ever experience. While her good looks should have made her popular, she was perceived as 'stuck up' and shunned by many of her classmates. The fact that she was the daughter of the High Priestess didn't help. Those that feared the coven avoided her like the plague; afraid they might say something to upset her and become the recipient of some dreadful curse. The girls belonging to her coven were jealous of her position, feeling they didn't stand a chance to reap the benefits bestowed upon her as daughter of their leader. That left very few with whom she could develop friendships and even those were superficial at best.

While her mother and sister continued to plan the upcoming event, Eliza poured hot water into the cup containing the special teabag. No one had noticed her slip the bag from the waistband of her pajama bottoms. Placing the cup and saucer in front of her mother, Eliza returned to the counter where she prepared hot cocoa for her sister and herself.

Leaving them to their business, Eliza then retreated to her room with her cocoa to get dressed.

Despite her apprehensions, Eliza was anxious to go outside and explore the old tool shed. Perhaps if she faced her fears head on she might find solace there rather than the confusing images and mixed emotions she encountered previously.

Pulling on heavy socks, she listened for any indication her spell might already be working. Disappointed, she made her way down the stairs, grabbing her parka and a pair of tall snow boots from the mudroom before entering the kitchen.

"Is it okay if I go outside?" She asked.

"Whatever for? Everything's covered with a sheet of ice." Helena responded. Once again she was annoyed by her youngest daughter.

"I just feel like going outside. I thought I'd look for my old sled. I think it's in the tool shed."

"Fine but don't be gone long, you might not have school, but you still have chores to do and you slept the whole morning away."

"I won't." Eliza promised, grabbing a flashlight out of the kitchen's junk drawer. With a little light she was certain the shed wouldn't feel so grim.

Crossing the field behind the house proved to be more difficult than she imagined. Although there was less than an inch of snow on the ground, it was covered by a thick layer of ice. Even the treads on her snow boots were no match for the slick surface and she found herself on the ground more than once as she picked her way across the field. When she finally arrived at the shed, she had to use a nearby rock to dislodge the frozen latch securing the door. Taking a deep breath to steady her nerves, she stepped inside the frigid building. Clicking on the flashlight she slowly scanned the interior. No larger than her family's sitting room, the shed housed an old work bench, stool, shelves built from discarded pallets as well as a rusty-legged card table and folding chair. Nothing about the building appeared out of the ordinary at first glance and Eliza wondered why it was her father spent so much time within its walls. No longer frightened by her surroundings, she made her way to the workbench to examine it closer.

As expected, it housed several old mason jars containing nails, screws, nuts and bolts. On the wall behind the bench was a pegboard where various tools were hung on hooks. Above the pegboard a piece of old barn wood served as a shelf housing a variety of motor oils, rusty car parts and the reel off an old fishing pole. Beneath the bench were several wooden crates containing discarded gardening tools, twine, broken clay pots as wells as stacks of old car magazines. The bench also contained a single drawer beneath its top and Eliza tugged at its handle to open it. To her surprise it sprung open without much effort and she withdrew its only contents, a leather-bond book about witches, witchcraft, occult, sorcery and demons. Eliza carefully opened the cover to find an image more horrifying than anything she had ever seen. The drawing depicted a naked woman atop an altar surrounded by a half dozen demon-like creatures, so grotesque they made her skin crawl.

The woman appeared to be screaming as the creatures tore at her flesh while her children huddled together witnessing the display. Despite her horror, she couldn't pry her eyes away from the image. Entranced she stood motionless until the shed door flung open and her sister ran inside.

"Come quick…something's wrong with Mother."

Eliza turned, staring blankly at her sister as if she couldn't comprehend her words.

"What's the matter with you? Come on." Anais tugged at her sister's arm, releasing her from the image's grip.

Eliza allowed her sister to drag her across the field, racing toward the house.

"She's having some sort of fit. I don't know if I should call an ambulance or one of the sisters." Anais debated, more to herself than to her younger sister.

Approaching the house they could hear their mother's wild cries and Anais quickly led the way, shielding Eliza behind her as they stepped into the kitchen. Wild-eyed and foaming at the mouth, Helena swatted at unseen attackers.

"They're everywhere, watch out, there's one on your face." Without warning, Helena lunged at Anais, slapping her so hard she fell backward, taking Eliza down with her.

"Mother, stop…stop! There's nothing there. Stop!" Anais cried out.

Eliza watched in shock as her mother grabbed a large kitchen knife and began thrusting it into the air, making jabs and slashing wildly at her imaginary attackers.

"Hide, Eliza, quick before she hurts you." Anais screamed, pulling her little sister up from the floor and pushing her toward the door. "Go to your room and lock the door."

Eliza ran as fast as she could go, tripping several times on her way up the stairs. Once in her room she fumbled with the lock before sinking to the floor and resting her back against it. As she listened in shocked horror her sister attempted to reason with their mother, who was clearly under the influence of the nightshade Eliza had laced her tea with.

"Mother, please! Stop, Mother, Stop! Anais screamed.

Then she heard a horrifying scream and she clasped her hands over her ears. As the cry, at first piercing, turned into a gurgling, choking sound, she withdrew her hands and waited. She waited, for what seemed an eternity for any sound that might indicate it was safe to come out. Finally she rose from the floor and cautiously opened her door enough to hear the frantic whispers of her mother. She could no longer hear her big sister and that scared her more than her mother's hysterical ramblings. As quietly as possible, she inched her way down the hallway toward her mother's room where she could call for help.

Down below, Anais struggled to remain conscious as the blood from her wounds pooled around her sprawled body. Wide-eyed she watched as her mother paced back and forth at her feet muttering nonsense about the devil's eyes watching her. If she could only get to the stove where a dishtowel hung from the oven door, she might be able to stop the bleeding. Cautiously she slithered sideways, keeping her eyes focused on her attacker. Each time she moved she had to stop and rest as her vision began to darken. She wasn't certain how much time had passed or whether or not Eliza had managed to get out of the house, but before she passed out she heard the sound of sirens approaching.

Eliza remained in her mother's room with her eyes on the locked door until she saw the police and rescue arrive. As soon as they pulled into the driveway, she bound out of the room and down the stairs, flinging wide open the door and practically knocking over the police officer as she rushed into his arms.

"Everything's going to be okay, sweetie. You go wait by my car while I check on your Mommy."

Eliza nodded her acknowledgement, but she refused to let go of the officer until he finally pried her away, handing her off to his partner who walked her down the steps and into the back seat of the police car. While his partner consoled the frightened child, the officer drew his weapon and cautiously made his way into the house, moving in the direction of Helena's voice. Five minutes later he exited the house with her in cuffs as the rescue workers rushed in to assist Anais.

Eliza watched in silence as her mother continued to wrestle with the officer, seemingly unaware of her surroundings and what was truly happening. When her sister was brought out of the house on a stretcher, Eliza attempted to run to her, but was stopped by the officer who was watching over her.

"You stay here, Sweetheart. Your sister is going to be just fine. What do you say we take a ride in my car and I'll show you around the police station?"

"Can't I go with Anais?" Eliza pleaded.

"No, Honey, the doctor needs to fix her up first. How about we get you something to eat? How does that sound?"

Eliza nodded in compliance, although she really wasn't hungry.

"Where are they taking my mother?"

"Don't you worry about that, she'll be looked after." The officer then looked over his shoulder, shielding the young girl's view as he watched a rescue worker sedate the hysterical woman.

Nearly three hours later, after Eliza ate a hamburger and fries and was being prodded with questions, Mrs. Putnam arrived.

"How would you like to come stay at our house for a couple of days?" She asked.

"I guess so." Eliza responded. "I'll have to ask my mother first though."

"I've already spoken to her, Honey. She said it would be fine." She assured her.

A look passed between her former teacher and the nice policeman that told Eliza they were keeping a secret.

"What about Anais?"

"She's going to be spending a couple of days in the hospital. We can go and visit her tomorrow if you'd like."

"Can't I see her now?"

"I'm afraid not, Honey. She's resting now, but I promise we'll visit first thing in the morning before you go to school."

Eliza considered protesting, but decided it was probably best not to make waves. Up until now she had managed not to draw attention to herself and she wanted to keep it that way. She hadn't been prepared for the fallout when the nightshade took effect and she was still reeling from the outcome. She had expected some kind of odd behavior on her mother's part, perhaps a one-sided conversation with a potted plant or even a fit of uncontrollable laughter, but she was ill prepared for such a violent outburst. She didn't know what the deranged woman saw, but whatever it was it scared her enough to stab her own daughter. Now Eliza had to deal with the consequences of her actions. Once her mother was rational she was certain to suspect foul play and she'd likely come to the conclusion that Eliza was responsible. If she didn't play her cards right, she might be at the mercy of Helena's wrath.

Chapter Six

Eliza remained at Mrs. Putnam's house for more than a week as doctors kept a watchful eye on Helena. When it had become apparent that her behavior was an isolated incident and the test results came back showing she had been poisoned, Helena insisted that she would handle the matter personally. Though the police department was adamant they would continue to work the case until the responsible party was apprehended, they all knew this was a problem likely to be placed on the backburner while the coven took matters into its own hands.

Much to Eliza's surprise, she wasn't even on her mother's radar. While Anais continued to recover at the hospital, Eliza was a constant at her mother's side. Whether it was either her guilty conscience or a need to be in the know, Eliza stuck to her mother like glue.

"Are you sure you're okay, Mother?" Eliza asked, searching her face for any signs of illness.

"I'm fine, Eliza, don't worry." She assured her daughter.

Eliza however insisted she take it easy and followed her mother around like a puppy dog.

Helena dealt with the annoyance by busying herself around the house and extended visits to the hospital. When Anais finally returned home, Helena no longer had any use for Eliza and any hopes she might have had that the incident might have somehow brought them closer were quickly dashed. Once again she was on the outside looking in, excluded from conversations and blatantly ignored. Anais had been an unintended victim of her revenge and Eliza sought to make it up to her by waiting on her hand and foot. Eliza sat with her sister for hours while she slowly recovered, keeping her entertained with board games, puzzles and pedicures.

The winter solstice plans had been tempered down in light of recent events so that Helena spent little time in preparation. Instead she focused her attention on Anais and finding out just who was responsible for poisoning her, an act of betrayal she intended to rectify.

Eliza had shamelessly eavesdropped on her mother's conversations with various members of the sisterhood, trying to stay ahead of whatever might come her way.

An emergency meeting was called and the watchers were challenged with the task of interviewing those they felt might have grudges against the High Priestess. Because the group had no one official meeting place, it was decided that the interviews would be held at the Lewis house, making it convenient for both Helena and Anais to be present.

One by one the members were paraded into the sitting room, to be grilled by the watchers. Eliza listened from above with her ear to an iron grate that served as an air vent in the old house. Each member was asked the same set of questions and each member denied any involvement. Only Eliza knew the truth and she planned on taking it to the grave with her. Finally when the interviews were complete and they were no closer to finding the guilty party, Helena made an announcement.

"If no one will come forward and admit their guilt, then all must be punished. We will purge this coven of any ambitions to relieve me of my post. Those that choose not to participate in the cleansing will then be stripped of their titles and expelled from our group forever."

That being said, Helena then ordered the watchers to inform the members of her decision and set to work preparing for the unfortunate task. Unlike her mother, Helena did not enjoy punishing her sisters. Though she did run a tight ship, often gravitating to old school methods, she preferred a more peaceful assembly. The fear her mother had invoked in her subordinates was something she worked hard to distance herself from, but it didn't come easy and she often found herself drawn to familiar albeit ruthless tactics.

While she demanded proper respect, she also encouraged her sisters to participate in nearly every decision.

Up in her room, Eliza moved away from the grate to consider what she had just heard. What sort of punishment did her mother have in mind? Was she going to spank the women? She giggled picturing Mrs. Pritchett bent over her mother's knee. *No*, she thought, *Mother most certainly has something far more sinister in mind.* On hands and knees she made her way over to the dresser where she retrieved the grimoire from its hiding place. Thumbing through the index, she looked for cleansing spells to prepare herself for whatever her mother intended to do. After reviewing a half dozen spells involving the cleansing of homes, spirits and past lives, she came upon an image of three women, their robes removed and lying at their feet, each bound at the wrists and ankles while another woman pierced their skin with a dagger. Eliza shivered in response to the image, which was detailed in vivid color. *Why is it that so many rituals involved the removal of the woman's clothes? Is it to make them more vulnerable or does the High Priestess just enjoy the sight of their naked form?* Another shudder ran through her body and she slammed the book closed, returning it to its hiding place.

By now Anais was able to move about the house with less difficulty, though she had not yet returned to school. Her mother insisted on keeping her home, not only until she was fully healed, but until such time as the gossip died down. The last thing she wanted was nosy teachers asking a lot of questions. Eliza was tasked with stopping by the high school each day to retrieve her sister's class assignments before coming home for the day. This meant she didn't arrive home until it was nearly dark and supper was on the table.

"Honestly, Eliza, you can't continue to doddle. We've been waiting fifteen minutes for you to come home. From now on if you're not home by the time I set the table, there won't be a place set for you."

"Sorry, Mother, the road was really icy so I had to walk slowly." Eliza apologized, furious that her efforts were chastised rather than appreciated.

Anais remained silent, afraid to anger her mother by coming to her sister's defense. Every since the stabbing she had grown fearful of her. Although her mother had claimed that she wasn't responsible for the attack, Anais couldn't help but think some underlying resentment might hide deep within. Many times she had caught her mother staring at her from across the room. Before the attack she had been flattered by the attention, but now she wondered if perhaps her mother might be jealous of her beauty.

Helena had once been a beautiful woman herself before years of hardship had made her grow hard. Her once creamy complexion was now riddled with age spots from too much time in the sun and her wavy locks, formerly shiny and black was peppered with wiry grays that made her appear much older than her age. Her formerly fit figure now bulged from her ill-fitting clothes and though once considered hip, wearing only the trendiest styles, Helena's wardrobe was now dated and the source of mean-spirited gossip amongst her peers.

"Is there something you'd like to say Anais?" Helena snapped, startling her daughter who hadn't realized she was staring at her.

"No, Mother," she whispered, returning her attention to her plate.

Helena was about to challenge her when the phone rang, distracting her.

"People just have no respect, calling in the middle of dinner."

Helena abruptly pushed back her chair, sending it toppling over on its side and stormed into the kitchen. Anais forced a smile and a wink at her younger sister to ease the tension. Eliza smiled back, grateful for the support. The two had just finished eating when Helena finally returned to the table.

"I have to run out for a bit. You two can clear the table and wash the dishes before you get started on your homework."

"Is everything okay now?" Anais cautiously asked.

"It's nothing for you to worry about, now go on."

With that she disappeared around the corner, collecting her handbag and keys before heading out the door. Both girls breathed a sigh of relief as soon as the door shut.

"What do you think that's all about?" Eliza wondered out loud.

"I have no idea, but if it gets her out of the house, it can't be all bad. Every since I came home from the hospital she watches me like a hawk. I swear she thinks I'm the one that poisoned her."

A nervous shutter went down Eliza's spine.

"Who do you think did it?"

"I honestly have no idea. It could have been anyone. Mother's convinced it's someone within the coven, but it could have been just about anyone. The way she shamelessly flirts with the men around town it wouldn't surprise me if it were someone's wife. Although the use of nightshade suggests it was someone involved in the practice."

Eliza nodded, avoiding eye contact with her sister as she scrapped the plates and stacked the silverware on top of the pile. As the conversation moved on to more trivial matters, Eliza couldn't help wonder what could have been so important that her mother left without finishing her dinner.

When it became obvious she was no longer involved in the conversation, Anais elbowed her.

"Hello...did you hear me?"

"Huh...what did you say?"

"I asked if you and Celeste have any plans for winter break."

"Oh, no, I mean we haven't really talked about it. We don't really hang out anymore." Eliza admitted.

"Really? What happened?"

For a split second Eliza actually considered confiding in her sister about her secret coven, but she wasn't completely certain she could trust her and the fear of her mother finding out was just too great of a risk.

"We just drifted apart. She doesn't really like my new friends."

"That's too bad, I know how close you two were. Well, who knows, things might change."

Eliza nodded, though she wasn't convinced. As far as she knew, Celeste didn't want anything to do with her or her newly formed coven. By the time they'd finished drying the dishes and made their way upstairs to their rooms to study, Eliza was certain whatever her mother was up to it had something to do with whatever punishment she intended to inflict on her sisters. She attempted to brooch the subject with Anais, but her sister was so uncomfortable with the topic, she evaded the question, instead delving into details about their upcoming winter solstice celebration. Her refusal to discuss the matter told Eliza she was not only privy to the particulars, but almost certainly would be participating in the sentencing.

Back in her room, Eliza made quick work of her assignments before shoving her books back into her bag and retrieving the now familiar grimoire. If she was going to prepare herself for whatever evil deed was about to be inflicted on the sisters, she had to consider every option available. By the time she finally closed the heavy book and returned it to its hiding place it was nearly ten o'clock and her mother had yet to return home.

As Eliza drifted off to sleep the wind howled outside her bedroom window. Like so many nights in the past, her dream world drew from her surroundings and she found herself wafting across an open field toward a dimly lit shed in the distance. As she slowly floated on an invisible cloud, she could hear the weeping of several women. The closer she got to the shed the more ragged the cries and she reached her arms as far as she could in an attempt to unlatch the door. Just out of her reach, the door banged open and closed as the force of the wind increased and she found herself clawing at the air as she sought to gain entrance. Pellets of ice and sleet flew through the air, grazing her face and arms. The sleeve of her nightgown caught on a loose shingle and finally she managed to maneuver herself through the tiny window of the shed. Inside, tall candles flickered, casting dark shadows on the faces of her mother's victims. Standing naked with the ankles and wrists bound, the women wore masks of shame. Each face resembled some form of grotesque disfigurement, intended to cause suffering. The first mask revealed bulging red eyes but when she lifted the mask the victim starred back at her through empty sockets, dark holes where her eyes should be were oozing black liquid. Despite her deformity, the woman's mouth was turned up in a cruel smile, while her eyebrows seemed to plead for mercy.

The second mask wore a sinister grin while underneath the victim's lips were sewn shut. In the palm of her hand she held her wriggling tongue.

The final victim's mask portrayed enormous ears hanging down to her shoulders.

Carefully she removed the mask to reveal bloody stumps where her ears should be. Terrified, she searched wildly for the women's attacker, slipping on the blood from their injuries. An eerie cackle reverberated from the darkest corner of the shed and she spun around to face it. Sickened by what she'd seen she began to lose consciousness and she struggled to stay focused. But, unable to control her movements she shuffled about the building knocking over candles and jars filled with various body parts, which crashed to the ground.

The sound of shattering glass startled her awake and she bolted out of bed in terror. As she struggled to separate her conscious mind from that of her nightmare, she focused on the storm raging outside her window. An icy blast struck her from behind and she spun around to see a large tree branch had broken through her window. Broken glass littered the floor along with pea-sized hail. Just as she was about to call out for help, her bedroom door flung open and her sister ran to her side.

"Are you okay?" She asked frantically, shaking Eliza out of her trance.

"I think so. What happened?"

Anais moved her stunned sister out of harm's way before responding. "That big old oak finally gave way. Let's try to clean up as best we can, then you can sleep with me tonight."

Eliza nodded, still in shock. "Where's Mother?"

"I don't know. I fell asleep, but I don't think she ever came home."

The girls set to work using towels to mop up the wet floors and shoving the broken glass into a pile. As the branch was far too large to remove on their own, they shoved blankets into the gap between the broken pane and the obstruction to prevent the freezing rain from entering the room. Satisfied they had done the best they could, they retreated to Anais' room.

"Are you okay?" Anais asked once more, stroking her little sister's hair.

"I had a nightmare. There were three women out in the shed being tortured, except it wasn't our shed, it was much bigger and I didn't recognize the women, but somehow I knew Mother was the one that hurt them."

"It was just a dream." Anais assured her.

"It really didn't feel like a dream. What will Mother do to the sisters? To punish them, I mean."

Anais hesitated, uncertain how much she should reveal to her little sister, if anything.

"Anais?"

"Nothing you should worry about, Eliza. The sisters are all strong women and they're committed to the coven. They're devoted to the practice and will do whatever is necessary to prove their loyalty to both the sisterhood and Mother. I promise whatever she decides it will be swift and just."

Eliza allowed her sister to cradle her in her arms as she drifted off to sleep, confident she would protect her from whatever action her mother intended.

Chapter Seven

Several days had passed since the big storm and no mention was made of where Helena had been that night or what had taken place. Unable to afford the services of a handyman or replace the window, Helena instructed the girls to saw the branch into smaller pieces so that they could easily remove it from Eliza's room and a damp piece of plywood from the basement was brought up to cover the empty window.

Anais was a constant at her mother's side and Eliza wondered whether or not she would honor her promise to keep her safe from whatever evil their mother intended. The guilt of her own actions kept her on pins and needles as the day of retribution grew closer.

Finally her mother announced the sisterhood would be holding assembly the following evening and Eliza needed to find somewhere else to be.

This was no easy task as she had few friends outside the dutiful members of her own coven, and they weren't exactly chomping at the bit to spend time with her. Ultimately though, it didn't really matter where she said she was going to be. She had no intention of actually leaving the property.

All she had to do was construct a believable scenario, enlisting one of her subordinates to help, and then double back undetected. Her classmate Annabel turned out to be the perfect choice. Following her home from school, Annabel assured Helena that it was okay for Eliza to spend the night at her house. Little concerned about her daughter's whereabouts so long as she was out of the way, Helena didn't bother to confirm with the girl's mother. Quickly throwing together an overnight bag, Eliza made her way out the door with her coconspirator and headed down the long driveway. Just in case her mother was watching, she walked Annabel down the road until she could no longer see the old house on the hill before thanking her and doubling back.

By the time she crept back into the house through the wooden bulkhead leading to the basement, it was already dark and the sisters were beginning to arrive. Eliza quietly made her way up the basement stairs, opening the door just a crack so she could hear what was being said.

In the sitting room, Helena had moved all the furniture to the back of the room, leaving a wide-open space to conduct the cleansing ritual. The watchers secured the two doorways leading in and out of the room while the remaining members of the coven, including Anais, knelt before their leader. Helena was dressed in a long black robe with a hood that concealed her face. Beside her was a tall table draped with a black cloth. Upon the table were various tools rarely seen by modern witches, though famously used by 17th century witch hunters. An uncomfortable silence fell upon the room as the women waited direction from their leader. Helena kept her back toward the assembly, focusing her energy to gather strength. A small part of her still clung to the images of her own childhood when she was tortured at the hands of her mother's coven and she fought to rid herself of any apprehensions that might make her appear weak in front of her subordinates. The only sound in the room was the anxious breathing of her puppets. Finally she turned and faced her minions.

"We are gathered here tonight under a veil of disloyalty. One among you has broken our sacred oath and betrayed not only me but also her sisters. I ask once again for the guilty party to step forward and admit her fault, sparing her sisters from what is to come."

Helena stood firm, her eyes shifting from one to the next, but all remained silent.

"So be it. It then falls on me to determine a punishment suitable for the crime. As I suffered, so shall you. Let it be known, I take no pleasure in this justice."

With that being said, she motioned for one of the watchers to bring forward Sarah Walcott. As Sarah slowly rose to her feet, her legs trembled beneath her. The watcher took her by the elbow and directed her to stand before their leader. Next it was indicated that she remove her robe so that she might stand naked with no secrets to hide. The blood rose in Sarah's cheeks as the assembly evidenced her nakedness.

Helena turned to the table, selecting a cat-of-nine tails.

"Turn and face your sisters." She instructed.

As Sarah turned, Helena swung the whip at the back of her knees causing her to drop to the floor and scream out in pain. As the watcher dragged her away, Helena addressed the group once more.

"Again I ask you; will the guilty party step forward?"

Once again the women were silent, rendered mute by their fear.

"Very well, bring me the next one." She instructed.

Once again the watcher stepped forward, approaching the women and pulling Celeste's mother to her feet. She was not about to go willingly.

"Priestess, with all due respect, I refuse to participate in such a barbaric punishment. It's one thing to expect loyalty from us, but quite another to whip us into submission."

Helena stood firm. "Does anyone else feel this way?"Slowly the women began to raise their hands as Sarah Walcott softly cried. Only Anais remained dutifully silent along with the watchers.

"I see…you are all here of your own free will and have given your solemn vow to follow my leadership, wherever that may lead you. That being said, if you choose to leave I will not stop you. Know that by doing so, you will no longer be a part of this coven."

Slowly several of the members lowered their hands, dropping their eyes to the floor.

Eliza strained to hear what was happening, frustrated by her confinement to the basement. From the top of the stairs she could only hear soft mutterings and the movement of what sounded like several people collecting their belongings. Unable to resist, she slowly opened the door wide, peering out in both directions. While the watchers were occupied escorting Mrs. Pritchett, Mrs. Putnam and Celeste's mother to the front door, she made her move, dashing to the back of the sitting room where she hid behind the back of the sofa.

Had her mother not returned to her punishments, she most certainly would have been spotted.

"Let us continue...again I ask for the guilty party to step forward and spare her sisters."

To Eliza and Helena's utter amazement, Anais rose.

"It was me." She announced softly, in a near whisper.

"If this is some sort of valiant effort to show mercy to your fellow sisters, it is a foolish move. The punishment will be not be amended because of our blood bond."

Anais straightened her back and took a deep breath. "I am responsible for poisoning you."

"For what purpose?" Helena demanded.

Anais hesitated briefly.

"Because I wanted to lead the coven."

Helena considered her words, avoiding the stunned look on her subordinate's faces. She refused to be judged by those of lesser standing than she.

"Very well...step forward."

Eliza clasped her hands over her mouth to keep from screaming out. Why would her sister admit to something she didn't do, knowing she would be punished severely? If she were braver she would stand up and shout in protest, admitting it was she not her sister that poisoned her mother's tea, but she was frozen in fear. She didn't need to witness Sarah Walcott's punishment to know it brought pain. If her mother inflicted that much pain to someone that might be responsible, what would she do to her sister? She didn't have to wait long to find out.

By now the watchers had returned to their posts and their leader summoned them forward. Helena instructed two of the women to hold her daughter's arms while the other two were given orders to secure her ankles as she lay on the floor. When the young girl was properly secured, her mother retrieved a box from beneath the table and placed it beside her.

Draped in black cloth to conceal its contents, the box seemed to vibrate with movement. Anais struggled to prepare herself. Her eyes searched her mother's face, looking for some sign of hesitation, but only saw conviction. Slowly, Helena removed the cloth and reached in cautiously.

"I find no pleasure in subjecting you to the tortures you inflicted on me. While my anguish was the result of hallucinations, to me they were as real as these."

From within the box, she produced one snake after another, placing each viper upon her daughter's writhing body. Anais cried out in terror as the snakes wrapped themselves around her.

Tears streamed down Eliza's face as she witnessed her sister tremble with crippling fear.

Helena seemed to be numb to her daughter's panic as she watched the snakes slither across her body. The more the girl struggled, the more aggressive the snakes became, biting at her flesh and wrapping themselves tightly around her bare extremities. Finally when she could take no more, Anais passed out.

Only then did the watchers release their hold on her and begin to collect the reptiles, carefully placing them back inside the box.

Eliza hiccupped back sobs, covering her mouth once more to stifle the sounds that would reveal her presence.

As Anais regained consciousness, the watchers lifted her from the floor and covered her with the white robe she was relieved of earlier. As her bleeding wounds came in contact with the robe, red stains spread across the fabric in a polka dot pattern. Unable to control her emotions, she sobbed loudly.

"Silence yourself, Anais. You have no one to blame but yourself." Helena spat.

Anais clutched her robe as she gingerly made her way back to her kneeling sisters.

"Tonight you have witnessed only a fraction of the nightmare I endured at my daughter's hands. Her betrayal is unforgivable. Because of her desire to remove me from power, she has broken her vow of loyalty and caused three of our sisters to leave our coven. It's with a heavy heart that I condemn her to a life of servitude without the possibility of promotion within this coven.

From this day forward, Sarah Walcott will sit at my side as maiden."

Still stinging from her earlier whipping, Sarah found it difficult to show appreciation for the recognition. However, out of respect to their leader, she whispered her gratitude.

Anais hung her head as if she were shamed by the demotion.

Only Eliza knew that what she had done was not only brave but also selfless, sparing her fellow sisters from the cruelty she had just endured.

As the meeting came to an end and the remaining members departed, Anais lingered still behind, knowing her punishment was not yet over. Eliza remained hidden from sight waiting for her opportunity to slip out of the room and back to the basement where she would spend the night.

When the last member had finally left and Helena closed and locked the door, Anais prepared herself for what was to come. If her mother could so easily torment her in front of an audience of her peers, what would she do when no one was left to witness her cruelty? As much as Eliza wanted to stay and protect her sister, her fear of being seen was far greater and she silently crept into the hallway on hands and knees. Once again safely behind the basement door, she placed her ear against the wood and waited. It took her mother less than a minute to pick up where she'd left off.

"My own flesh and blood! You'll pay dearly for the humiliation you've caused me. I've spent my entire life preparing for the day I would lead this coven to greatness, surpassing anything the Lewis clan has ever done. And now...now you have pulled the rug out from under me. Undermined my authority. Tarnished my good name. And for what?"

Tears streamed down Anais' face as she braced herself. "I'm sorry." She whispered.

"Sorry! You're sorry! Believe me, Anais, you'll be more than sorry. You'll rue the day you put your selfish ambitions ahead of this family. As long as I breathe, I will make it my mission to destroy you as you've destroyed me. Now go to bed, I can't bear to look at you."

Chapter Eight

The winter passed slowly in the Lewis home with Helena determined to keep her promise to make Anais' life a living hell. Anais's room was stripped of everything except the bare necessities. Not only did she take away her posters, record player and *Teen Magazines*, but also her makeup, hair accessories and favorite clothes; replacing them with unflattering garments from Goodwill. Fearful she would skip school rather than be seen by her peers; Helena drove her to school each day and watched as she entered the building before returning home. This left Eliza alone in the house long enough to read a little every day from the family grimoire.

Any guilt she had felt for putting her mother through the terrifying hallucinations died the night she witnessed her sister's horrible ordeal and she made a vow to rid themselves of the monster they called 'Mother' once and for all. While she had no intentions of revealing the fact that she was the one responsible for poisoning Helena, her gut told her Anais suspected as much. If she did know and chose to suffer to protect her, the least she could do was repay her kindness.

Helena attempted to distract the remaining members of the coven by giving them each new assignments, hoping to take focus off her. Each sister was tasked with recruiting new members, who would be sworn in during the spring solstice celebration. Because recruiting was no easy task, the coven met twice a week to discuss strategies and present potential candidates. Despite her busy schedule, Helena still managed to keep dominance over Anais and was unrelenting in her punishments.

Helena found it particularly entertaining to make Anais act as servant to the coven of which she was technically no longer a member. Until she felt her daughter was trustworthy enough to be left alone, the bi-weekly meetings were held at the Lewis house. On those evenings Eliza stayed up in her room as instructed, but kept her ear to the floor so that she could continue to monitor what was going on below.

The meetings themselves were less than exciting and Eliza wondered whether her mother was attempting to regain the sisters' trust and respect after losing so many members as a result of her antiquated ways. Anais obediently served the women, ever keeping her eyes focused on the floor as a sign of submission. When a subject of interest occasionally caught her ear and she looked up out of instinct, her mother would immediately send her to the kitchen to fetch a fresh bottle of wine.

Sarah Walcott seemed to be flourishing in her new position as maiden to the High Priestess and Helena praised her continuously, if for no other reason than to inflict further shame on her daughter. If anyone else saw through the façade, no mention was made of it; at least not inside the Lewis household.

Eliza's own coven was growing by leaps and bounds as more and more candidates were inducted into the fold. While most of the girls were friends of current members, Eliza hand-picked a couple herself. Those that she chose received the most important positions, as they were less likely to attempt to unseat her. She had little trust for anyone who sought out membership.

Each new candidate went through a rigorous training program before they could be officially initiated into the coven. Not only were they required to educate themselves with basic spell casting, but they were also expected to prove their loyalty to the sisterhood by performing an act of selflessness, something Eliza herself knew little about. Needless to say, most of the candidates chose acts that in some way benefited Eliza. One girl gave up her date to a school dance, insisting the boy take Eliza in her place, while another risked getting caught shoplifting to acquire a pair of teardrop earrings in which Eliza had showed interest. While no outright disapproval was shown toward these acts, some of the members secretly wondered about the direction in which the coven was heading.

Whenever possible Eliza called a meeting to reconfirm the group's commitment to the sisterhood. This was mainly done on the weekend when they could convince their parents they were just hanging out at each other's house. If experience had taught them anything it was that sooner or later they were certain to be found out, so they made the most of their time while they could. On an unusually warm March day, Eliza called her sisters to meet inside an old railcar tucked behind the old train station along an abandoned track. The railcar was a place to hide away from prying adults and local authorities. Generally it was used for the purpose of concealing teens drinking and smoking, but on occasion couples used it as a place to make out and for that reason it became legendary to most of Wells' youth.

As the group settled in, Eliza went over the day's agenda. "I called this meeting to reconfirm everyone's commitment to our coven. I've been hearing whispers in the hallways at school about what goes on at our private meetings so someone must be blabbing."

A nervous shudder went through the group as their leader starred down at her subordinates through squinted eyes. While each of the girls averted her eyes after first meeting Eliza's stare, only one refused to look her in the face. Damiana was a recent inductee, who had been chosen by the coven's longtime member Morgan. A seventh grader whose popularity had stemmed from her beauty, Damiana had been a welcomed candidate with potential to bring recognition and respect to an otherwise shunned group of misfits. As her sponsor, Morgan was responsible for teaching her the ways of the coven as well as seeing that she obeyed the bylaws set forth by their leader. Now, seeing Eliza focus in on her underling, Morgan nervously chewed her fingernails.

"It seems pretty obvious who the guilty person is. Damiana, step forward." Eliza commanded.

The girl rose timidly, looking to her sisters for reassurance, but was shocked when one by one they shifted, turning their backs to her in unified support of their leader. A tear streamed down her face and she hung her head in shame. Again Eliza addressed her.

"Do you deny revealing our coven's secrets?"

Damiana shook her head without speaking.

"Your sisters can't hear you."

"No." Damiana choked in between sobs.

"What do you have to say for yourself?"

"I meant no harm…I'm proud to be a chosen
member. It will never happen again."

"You will step outside while your sisters and
I discuss your punishment."

Damiana ran from the train car, sobbing
uncontrollably as the door closed behind her. The
other members turned once more to face their
leader.

"Morgan, you are her sponsor so it's your
responsibility to administer punishment. What do
you suggest?"

Morgan considered the options, knowing
nothing short of cruelty would satisfy their leader.

"We make her a mute. Outside of class and
home she is not allowed to speak until the Spring
Solstice."

Eliza lips curled up in a vicious smile,
pleased with the response.

"Do we all agree?"

The girls agreed in unison.

"Very well, bring her back in."

Morgan left to retrieve her underling while
Eliza continued with the business at hand.

"Now that the unfortunate business is settled I have a personal request."

Morgan returned followed by Damiana and judging from her somber mood it was evident she had been told her punishment. Eliza waited until the two settled in before she continued.

"For some time now my mother has been punishing Anais for something she didn't do. I've sat by and watched my sister suffer in silence, hoping she might grow a backbone and defend herself, but it seems clear she is either unable or unwilling to challenge my mother. Very little affects my mother because her powers are strong. That is why I need your help."

The group shifted, clearly on edge.

"The only way she will give up leadership and control over our community is through shame. I saw of glimpse of it when she was poisoned. She was so embarrassed by that ordeal she found it difficult to leave the house. If we can find a way to tarnish her reputation, the sisterhood just might turn their backs on her. Does anyone have any suggestions?"

There was a brief pause while each of the girls thought it over, followed by a frenzied outburst of childish suggestions.

"You could make her hair fall out."

"You could give her laxatives so she has diarrhea."

"You could turn the furniture upside down and make her think there's a poltergeist in your house."

Eliza held up her hand to stop the nonsense. "She's not a kid, none of those things will work. She'll know I did it and besides, that wouldn't shame her. It has to be something that everyone in town will find out about."

Once again the group fell silent as they tried to come up with a conceivable solution. Whether it was the shared focus on the subject or merely an oversight on her part, Eliza realized the answer had been staring her in the face all along.

"Why didn't I think of it before?" She asked out loud.

A fury of "what's" filled the rail car as they perked up.

"What makes my mother so powerful in the first place?"

The girls looked to each other for the answer.

"The Lewis name. It's the Lewis name that commands respect and puts the fear in everyone's mind. So what if the name that she was so proud of were somehow tarnished?"

"How?" Morgan chirped up.

"What if she thought that a story was going to come out that made a mockery out of the Lewis name? She would be so embarrassed she wouldn't be able to face her sisters or the community."

While her peers considered Eliza to be wise beyond her years, the group collectively doubted she had the wherewithal to pull off such an enormous deception. Eliza, however, was not to be detoured and she dismissed the group so she could focus on coming up with a good plan. One way or another she planned on taking her mother down.

Taking a shortcut to get home, Eliza quickly ran with determination, eager to get back home and dig through the attic for anything that might bring shame to her mother. She had no idea what that item might be, but that didn't stop her from fantasizing about the look on her mother's face when the news hit her. To her delight, Helena was nowhere in sight when she returned home and the house was eerily quiet. Thinking her sister might be interested in joining her, she climbed the stairs two at a time, calling out Anais's name. By the time she reached the top of the stairs, Anais was waiting for her, outside her bedroom door.

"What's the matter?" She asked nervously.

"Nothing…is Mother here?"

"No, she went to Kennebunkport for some supplies. She probably won't be back home until dinner."

"Good…follow me." Eliza instructed, while dragging her sister by the arm.

"I'm not going anywhere until you tell me what's going on."

"Okay fine. Have you ever heard Mother talk about anyone in the Lewis family doing something she might not be so proud of?"

"I don't know. Why?"

"Because I just thought of the perfect way to get you out of trouble."

Once again, Eliza pulled Anais by the arm toward the attic steps as she explained what she intended to do.

"If she finds out you're behind this, there's no telling just what she might do to you." Anais cautioned.

"Let me worry about that. Besides, if my plan works the way I think it will, I don't believe she'll be in any position to punish anyone."

Anais stopped midway up the staircase. "It was you that poisoned her, wasn't it?"

Eliza met her sister's eyes. "Yes...I'm so sorry for everything you've been through. I was there when you said it was you. I should have stood up and accepted responsibility but I was too scared. That's why I've been working so hard to make it up to you. I won't stop until she pays for everything she's done."

Anais reached out to her little sister, taking her by the shoulders and bringing her in for a hug. "I would do anything to protect you. You know that. I couldn't stand there and watch innocent people pay for what they didn't do. She's sick, you know. Nobody in their right mind would do the things she's done."

"I think she killed our father." Eliza wept.

"Come on…we need to stay focused. There's an old trunk up here I've seen. It must be at least a hundred years old."

Together they made their way up the few remaining stairs and into the cold attic. A shudder ran through Eliza's body and she hesitated at the threshold. Her pause did not go unnoticed by Anais and she squeezed her hand to reassure her. Eliza managed a weak smile as she followed her sister into the belly of the attic. Over the years the spacious attic seemed to grow smaller as more and more of their mother's possessions made their way into the graveyard of memories.

As she looked around, Eliza recognized items belonging to their father cast haphazardly amongst the remnants of their ancestor's lives. While Eliza lingered in reflection, Anais moved to the back wall where the oldest of their relation's belongings were stored. Amongst a collection of steamer trunks and cedar chests was a leather trunk with brass hinges. The Lewis family crest engraved into the lid of the chest set it apart from the others.

"Over here." Anais announced, dropping to her knees to examine the trunk more closely.

Eliza shook off her hesitation and ran to her sister's side just in time to see her open the heavy lid. At first glance the trunk appeared to contain little more than a collection of old garments, however, after removing the items they discovered a false bottom. A chill of anticipation ran up Eliza's spine as her sister carefully removed the wooden board. To their disappointment, the only item beneath the board was a yellowed and moth-eaten wedding gown dating back to the Victorian era. Not to be detoured, the girls moved on – opening one trunk after another until they had exhausted all possibilities. Other than a handful of disturbing photos depicting a number of deceased relatives, the girls found little of interest.

"Well that's it." Anais announced. "I was sure we'd find something."

"We can't give up." Eliza pleaded. "There must be something we can use."

"We can keep looking, Eliza, but my guess is that if there was anything that might embarrass her, she probably already destroyed it."

The girls continued their search until the sun set and they heard their mother's car pull into the driveway. By the time Helena entered the house, the girls were in their respective rooms with their schoolbooks open and pencils in hand.

Chapter Nine

Several weeks passed by while the Lewis sisters continued their search efforts. By now they had exhausted their efforts in both the attic and the basement and had also begun the tedious task of examining their mother's papers scattered about the house. Although she maintained extensive logs concerning the activities of the coven, they found little in the way of family history.

"It doesn't make sense." Anais thought out loud.

"What?" Eliza asked looking up from a stack of loose papers she was rifling through.

"For someone so proud of her family name you would think she would have an abundance of ancestral history. It doesn't make sense that we can't find one single document."

Eliza agreed. "She must have a secret hiding place we haven't found."

The girls continued their search, continually listening for the familiar sound of the family station wagon. On several occasions over the next weeks they were nearly caught and they had to scramble to clean up; often times shoving books and papers under the sofa just as their mother walked in the door. Helena had grown suspicious of the girls, who up until recently had very little to do with each other. She had actually confronted Anais with her suspicions.

"You and your sister seem to be rather chummy lately. What brought that on?"

"I don't know. I guess now that she's getting older we have more in common." Anais lied.

The truth was, they really couldn't be more different. While Anais had always been proud to sit at her mother's side, silently hoping she would never have to step up and lead the coven; Eliza wanted nothing more than to overthrow her mother and run the coven the way she saw fit. Now that neither sister had any affiliation with the sisterhood, other than their mutual desire to bring shame to their abusive mother, they lead very different lives.

Outside of the home, Anais concentrated on her studies and social activities. Like many of the local teenagers, Anais liked to hang out at the beach and party in the woods. At fifteen she had already lost her virginity, something she regretted almost immediately. Her natural good looks made her the desire of every boy in school.

Eliza, on the other hand, shied away from boys – not that they were busting down her door; concentrating all her efforts on her coven and on revenge against her mother. Although Anais tried to convince her, she didn't give herself enough credit that boys would eventually come to see her inner beauty. At only eleven, Eliza had resigned herself to the notion she would forever be alone.

Helena dropped the subject although she was convinced there was more to their newly found friendship than either was willing to admit. Never did she suspect it had anything to do with her, in fact quite the opposite. Helena suspected that the girls were collaborating on a joint mission to build their own coven. While it irked her to no end that the girls would go behind her back rather than ask for her assistance, she gave them credit for their determination and spirit.

By late May, Helena's coven was now back on track and she was also confident enough in her followers to suggest they conduct a special ritual.

"I have gathered you here tonight with great news. I have been blessed with a vision from the Goddess herself. She came to me in a dream, bringing word of a child, not yet born, that will lead us to greatness. The child bears the mark of our coven and possesses all of the power of our combined ancestors. Through this child, we shall dominate the elements and she will bring peace and tranquility to all those among us."

A collective gasp rang out amongst the sisterhood as the members excitedly bombarded their leader with questions. Helena raised her hand to silence the women.

"Who among you is willing to participate in the ritual? I have called upon a coven of warlocks who are willing to share their seed with any who wish to conceive."

A look of trepidation passed across the faces of the group. While they had grown accustomed to disrobing in front of their sisters as part of their solstice and initiation ceremonies, they had never involved their male counterparts.

"Now is not the time to be timid. Only through sacrifice do we gain riches."

The women, however, required much further convincing and they inundated their leader with questions.

"Where will the ritual take place?"

"Will it be dark?"

"Will everyone witness our coupling?"

Again, Helena raised her hand to silence the women.

"I assure you that the ritual will be both seductive and beautiful at the same time. In order to ensure a successful outcome, the ritual will take place at midnight on the eve of the next full moon.

The two covens will join together at the meadow with only the light of the moon to guide us. An elixir will be passed amongst the participants to remove inhibitions and heighten the experience."

Some of the younger members giggled aloud, showing their immaturity. Helena glared in their direction.

"What I'm suggesting is no joke, ladies. Great responsibility and commitment comes with this child. You will not have the father's aide in raising the child, only that of the coven. Though you will bear the child and be responsible for her care, the child will belong to the sisterhood to do with her as we see fit."

"But how can we ensure it will be a girl?" Sarah asked, speaking for the first time.

"My vision was quite clear about that. Should the coupling produce a child without the markings or the proper sex, then it is not the chosen one."

The women sat in silence considering the possibilities. On one hand they might potentially spawn the most powerful witch the world had even known, but on the other they might simply become the single parent of an unwanted, fatherless child. This was particularly upsetting to those members who were married and had husbands to consider.

"I will give you all time to think it over. This is not something you should take lightly. We will meet again at the end of the week for your decision."

Unaware her girls were listening upstairs; Helena described what would take place in detail. While Eliza found the very notion of such an act revolting, Anais was quite intrigued. By the time the coven parted ways, Anais had already made up her mind she would attend the gathering, hidden amongst the shadows where she could watch without fear of being seen.

With the ritual only two weeks away, Helena was too busy preparing to notice anything the girls might be up to. Satisfied she knew what they were doing anyway, she loosened the reigns just a bit, allowing the girls to venture from the house as long as they were together and returned before dark.

Convinced they had searched every square inch of the house, Anais suggested they check out the town archives hoping they might locate something in the families' past that might tarnish its reputation. Although young Eliza was less than thrilled at the prospect of spending countless hours scanning old newspapers on microfiche in a musty library basement, she conceded they had run out of options.

Day after day the duo sat side by side at the machines scanning documents until their eyes were blurry and red. Eliza complained continually that the small print and moving pages made her sick to her stomach, but Anais encouraged her on. Finally when they had both nearly given up hope of finding anything, Anais jumped up.

"That's it."

"What? What is it?" Eliza scanned the page for whatever had caught her sister's attention. "I don't see anything."

"Exactly. There should at least be a record of Mother's birth, but there isn't."

"So...maybe they didn't make an announcement."

"That's just it. The hospital posted the announcements back then of all the babies born each week. So if she was born here, there should be a record of her birth. There are only three girls listed and none to the Lewis family."

Eliza tried to understand what her sister was trying to say.

"Don't you see? It's just that she must have been adopted." Anais explained.

"But if she was adopted she isn't a Lewis."

"Exactly." Anais waited for her little sister to digest the news.

"If she's not a Lewis then neither are we."

"That's just it. Her influence comes from everyone's belief that she's a descendant of the powerful Lewis bloodline. Once they know the truth she'll no longer have that fear to hold over the coven and my guess is that they will quickly remove her as High Priestess."

Eliza considered everything her sister was saying. Like her mother, she too had used her name to influence her subordinates into doing whatever she desired. If it became common knowledge that the Lewis line had died with the aunt she'd never known, her quest to lead the most powerful coven the world had ever known would die as well. Somehow she had to find a way to bring down her mother, but without revealing her secret.

"Do you think she knows she was adopted?"

"She must…perhaps not as a child, but she would have had to see her birth certificate at some point." Anais reasoned.

"Do you think Father knew? Maybe that's why she killed him, to keep him or anyone else from finding out."

"We don't know for sure she killed him, Eliza. We only know he got sick. His illness could have been caused by anything."

"You don't really believe that, do you?"

"I used to. There was a time I would have believed her incapable of inflicting harm on any other human being. But now…now I'm not sure there is a limit to her cruelty. I don't think anything is beyond her."

"I think she poisoned him." Eliza stated with certainty.

The girls sat in silent thought for several minutes while they considered what to do next.

"If she was adopted and Father found out, he likely would have confronted her. If there was any evidence, I'm sure she destroyed it."

"Maybe not." Eliza said, grabbing her sister by the hand and pulling her up. "Remember how he used to spend hours in the old tool shed? If he were going to hide something it would be in there. We've searched the whole house and we didn't find anything."

Anais smiled broadly. "You're pretty smart for a kid, you know."

Eliza beamed. "Let's hurry. We don't have much time before dark."

The girls were breathless from running by the time they reached the dilapidated shed, which sat eerily silent before a border of evergreens. Both hesitated as they stepped inside, fearful of any creatures that might be roaming about in the abandoned building. Being more familiar with her surroundings, Eliza took the lead, reaching up to the shelf above the workbench to retrieve an old oil lantern, which she promptly lit with a match from a box on the bench.

"I can't remember the last time I was in here. I couldn't have been more than seven years old." Anais whispered nervously.

"I've come out here a few times since Father died. It's the only place I feel his presence."

Anais nodded, understanding how her sister might feel closer to their father amongst his things.

"There's not much in here. What makes you think he might hide something out here?"

"The first time I came here I found a book that seemed out of place. I think he might have been doing some research."

Eliza fumbled through the bench's drawer, retrieving the old book, which she handed to her sister. While Anais thumbed through the pages, Eliza continued to search about the shed for anything that might hold a secret hiding place. She rummaged through a half dozen old cigar boxes as well as a barrel of empty potato sacks before she settled on the floor to browse through the boxes of magazines. She was reaching under the workbench to retrieve the second box when a gust of wind pushed against the building forcing a draft through a small opening in the wall. Eliza strained her eyes for a closer look.

"Hand me the lantern." She called out.

Anais obliged, joining her sister on the floor.

"What is it? Did you find something?"

"I'm not sure." Eliza responded, shoving aside the remaining boxes to expose the wall.

"There's a draft over here and it looks like..." She stopped midsentence as her hand came in contact with the edge of the false wall and a small cupboard was revealed. Anais moved in closer for a better look.

"You were right." Anais squeezed her little sister's shoulder.

Eliza took a moment to soak in her sister's acknowledgement before reaching into the small cupboard and retrieving a bundle of papers bound with a piece of rawhide. She barely noticed the bump to her head as it came in contact with the underside of the workbench as she scrambled to her feet, flinching briefly before bringing her attention back to the discovery.

"Let me see." Anais insisted, relieving her sister of the bundle.

Amongst the stack of worn and faded papers was a copy of the deed to the house, which they had already seen amid their mother's papers; as well as an old faded copy of each of the girls' birth certificates, titles to cars long ago sent to the junk yard and receipts for unknown purchases. Within a folded manila envelope was an unused train ticket dated the year their father had died. Anais studied it closely.

"What is it?" Eliza asked, leaning in closer.

"I think Father was planning on leaving before he got sick. It's a train ticket to Boston."

Anais struggled to hold back tears as a knot in her throat threatened to choke her. She had never considered her father might leave them. She hadn't been blind to the problems in her parent's marriage, but still, that he had actually purchased a train ticket and planned to leave was devastating. Eliza nudged her sister who seemed to be lost in thought.

Taking a deep breath to clear her head, Anais continued to make her way through the stack of papers, looking for anything that might indicate he knew their mother's secret. Finally she reached the bottom of the pile.

"Well, that's it. There's nothing here."

"There has to be. Why would he hide that stuff unless he was afraid she would find it?"

Anais shook her head. "I just don't know. Maybe we're wrong, maybe she wasn't adopted. There could be a simple explanation as to why her birth wasn't announced."

"Like what?" Eliza challenged.

"I don't know. Maybe she was sick when she was born and they didn't think she was going to make it. Maybe they had enemies and they didn't want them to know a daughter was born and they asked the hospital not to announce it."

Eliza dove back under the bench once more, feeling her way into the cupboard in hopes she might have missed something. Disappointed and frustrated she began to cry.

Anais knelt down beside her, offering her support. "Don't worry, we still have time to figure something out. She won't get away with what she's done and if she really is responsible for our father's passing, I'll make sure she rots in hell."

Eliza clung to her sister as if her very life depended on it. Never had she needed her support more than now, when she felt so hopeless. Perhaps the weight of so many years of hatred for her mother had simply become too much to bear on her own, or maybe she was just tired. Tired from a lifetime of deception. Tired of pretending to be someone she wasn't. Her determination had always been enough to see her through the most difficult times, but now it all seemed so pointless. She had invested too much of herself into a cause without resolution and now she had nothing else. If she didn't have revenge, if she couldn't avenge her father's death and betray her mother, what purpose did she have? Anais had only just come to realize the evil within their mother, but she had known it all along. She had struggled for years while the truth ate away the hope she had of any normalcy. While her sister made friends and enjoyed her teenage years, she fought an unseen battle in solitude.

"Let's go back to the house. Mother will be home soon and we need to make sure our chores are done."

Eliza wiped her tears, allowing her sister to help her up from the floor. As they made the trek across the overgrown field to the house, Anais reminded her sister of happier times when their father would pitch a tent in the field on warm summer nights and they would sleep out amongst the stars to the sounds of crickets chirping and the distant sound of waves crashing against the rocky beach. Of nights when they could hear the sound of the train's whistles and the foghorns blowing to signal the ships into port. On those nights he would fill their heads with tales of hobos and pirates until they fell asleep in his arms.

Eliza smiled, remembering how much their father loved them.

For Anais, recalling those moments from long ago only confused her more. *Why would a man who loves his children so much, purchase a train ticket to leave them?* The more information they found, the less sense it seemed to make.

While the girls went through the motions of completing their chores, neither mind drifted far from the mystery surrounding their father's death and whatever secret their mother kept.

Anais was still convinced their mother was not of the Lewis clan and had somehow managed to keep that information from anyone that might use it against her. She wondered whether her father was the only resident of Wells to meet an untimely death. From everything that she'd seen during her time in the coven, nothing would surprise her.

Eliza continued to choke back her tears of frustration, reminding herself how many years she had invested in pursuit of revenge.

Helena returned home just a little after dark, satisfied to see that the girls were home and their chores were completed.

Anais noted her particularly chipper mood, growing even more suspicious. Lately she found herself dissecting her mother's every word and action as if her very life depended on it. Whether she truly was up to something or she was just in a heightened state of awareness she couldn't be certain; but she understood for the first time how isolated Eliza must have felt all those years when she alone carried the weight of suspicion.

"Anais, you're positively glowing tonight. To what do you attribute your rosy cheeks? I hope you're not coming down with something."

Anais touched her cheeks in response. "I feel fine, Mother. Perhaps I spent a bit too much time in the sun today."

Helena squinted her eyes as if in doing so she might get a glimpse into her daughter's mind.

Anais fidgeted nervously in anticipation of further questioning, but her mother simply turned, making her way into the kitchen.

"Where's your sister?" Helena called over her shoulder.

"I'm right here, Mother." Eliza announced, depositing the broom and dustpan into the closet before relieving her mother of the bag of groceries she was carrying.

"Wonderful. I was thinking we might make sundaes after dinner tonight. How does that sound?"

Both Anais and Eliza put on a cheerful front, feigning excitement. The trio ate dinner in virtual silence, eager to be done with the formality before moving on to dessert.

With her suspicions, Anais found it difficult to participate in idle chitchat and her lack of contribution to the evening's conversation did not go unnoticed.

"Anais, whatever has you so preoccupied this evening? Is there something you'd like to talk about?"

"No, I guess I'm just tired. Everything is fine, really."

Helena stared at her daughter for a moment before giving up.

"Alright, but I hope you know you can talk to me about anything. No subject is off-limits as far as we're concerned. I'd like to think you'd come to me if you were in any kind of trouble."

"Of course, Mother."

Eliza watched the exchange with detached interest, neither buying her mother's sudden compassion or concern that her sister might spill the beans on their little investigation. Her thoughts were focused on figuring out what to do next. Now that it appeared unlikely she would ever find evidence regarding her mother's paternity, it was imperative that she come up with a new plan.

Chapter Ten

As the eve of the coupling ritual drew ever
nearer, several members of the coven expressed
their concerns. Not only was the ceremony rare in
modern times—most members having never heard
of such a thing—but its affiliation with the dark
arts made those eligible to participate more than a
little nervous. Several of the women speculated
whether or not Helena's motivation to perform the
ceremony had less to do with her vision and more
with regards to her control over the coven. The
women that had served under her the longest had
doubts whether her vision was real at all. In all the
years they had practiced the craft, she had never so
much as discussed the gift of visions. It seemed
rather convenient that a vision should come now,
when she was attempting to regain the support of
the coven. There also was the matter of the actual
coupling. Would she hold it over all those who

participated as a method of blackmail, using the act as a way to shame the women into doing her bidding?

On the evening before the ritual was to take place, Helena called a meeting in order to discuss the particulars of the ceremony as well as prepare the costumes for the vessels.

"In preparation of the ceremony, we will perform a cleansing ceremony for those that wish to participate in the coupling. Let us join together in prayer as we cleanse our sisters."

Amongst the six members who had offered their bodies was Sarah Walcott. Sarah was the first to step inside the circle and remove her robe, exposing her naked body. Her nervousness did not go unnoticed by those tasked with purifying her.

Likewise, Helena observed the young girl's hesitation and immediately she acted to avert a domino effect amongst the women.

"It's quite natural to feel nervous as we draw nearer to the hour of conception. Tell us, Sarah, have you ever laid with a man before?"

Sarah shyly shook her head, keeping her eyes on the floor.

"How lovely then for you that you should choose to lose your innocence amongst those most dear to you and for the greater good of the coven. You are a fine example of the sacrifice we all must make in order to achieve greatness."

The circle tightened around her, each of the women offering their gratitude at her willingness to participate. Helena smiled as two additional members announced their desire to join in the ceremony. After cleansing each of the women, the group moved to the kitchen where they prepared flower wreaths that the women would wear upon their heads. The wreaths would be the only articles the women would wear. Next, a special ink was prepared that would be used to draw the symbol of the pentagram on the bellies of the women. Once again the coven formed a circle and one by one the sisters were tattooed.

Upstairs Anais and Eliza listened through the grate in the floor, every once in a while catching a glimpse of the women as they passed back and forth.

Eliza bombarded her sister with questions about the coupling, which Anais responded to with vague answers that only confused her more.

"Are you really going to go watch? It sounds disgusting."

Anais shrugged absently.

"What if Mother sees you?"

"I'll be careful, don't worry."

Anais slept only a little that night, tossing and turning and eventually falling asleep only to be awoken by nightmares that were so vivid she had to remind herself they were dreams. The dreams centered around the coupling ceremony, which seemed to drag on forever. From where she hid she could see little of what was happening, but was afraid to move any closer. The sound of chirping crickets was so loud they drowned out the distant chanting of the coven. The tall grass was alive with insects and night crawlers going about their normal nightly business, undisturbed by her presence. The flickering light of a bonfire at the center of the ceremony sent hot ambers into the night sky and despite her lengthy distance from the gathering, an occasional fragment landed on her body, burning through her skin.

Finally her curiosity got the better of her and she slowly made her way through the tall grass on her hands and knees. With her senses on high alert she quickly became aware of the presence of someone in her proximity. When she turned to look, a bag was placed over her head and she was dragged, kicking and screaming by her arms toward the center of the circle. She could feel a dozen hands tearing at her clothing as she was stripped naked.

Unable to see through the bag, she trembled as snakelike fingers slid across her body while a crowd of watchers shrieked with enthusiasm. Just when she thought she could bear it no more, the bag was pulled from her head and she came face to face with her mother.

"Anais…Anais wake up. You're having a nightmare."

The frightened girl shrank away from her mother; unsure whether she was real or part of her nightmare.

Annoyed by her daughter's lack of gratitude for saving her from whatever images haunted her subconscious, Helena removed herself from the bed.

"I have a very important day tomorrow and I need my rest. See to it I'm not disturbed again."

Helena stormed out of her daughter's room, leaving the teenager confused and clutching her covers. By the time she finally drifted back to sleep she was more determined than ever to figure out whatever secret her mother kept buried away. Only a monster could be so uncaring. Her only regret was that she hadn't seen it earlier and spared her sister years of pain and solitude. Her own heart broke for little Eliza. To Anais, Eliza was beautiful and innocent, not the black sheep her mother made her out to be. Without their father to intervene, Eliza hadn't stood a chance.

Whether it was merely her subconscious working overtime or a higher power shining light on an otherwise dark avenue, she couldn't be certain, but when Anais woke up the following morning she knew exactly what to look for.

Helena left the house early to make last minute preparations for the coupling ceremony. Both Anais and Eliza watched her from the small ventilation window in the musty attic until they could no longer see their mother's car and were certain it was safe to begin their search.

"I don't understand we already looked up here." Eliza moaned, uncomfortable with the thought of digging into boxes where small creatures might be nesting.

"I had a dream last night or maybe it was an old memory I just recalled. Either way, I'm sure we'll find what we're looking for behind grandma's portrait."

Anais tugged at a heavy old steamer trunk, dragging it into the center of the attic. Next, with Eliza's assistance she inched an old wardrobe away from the wall until she was able to reach behind it and retrieve the long forgotten portrait of Helena's mother.

Eliza shivered with anticipation as Anais placed the large frame face down on the attic floor.

Anais took a deep breath and squeezed her sister's hand. Carefully she tore away the paper backing that protected the canvas until she found what she was looking for.

"It's here. I must have seen Mother put it here when I was little and forgot about it until last night."

Eliza moved in closer. "Let me see."

Anais removed the manila envelope and unwound the string closure. With one last look at her sister, she reached into the envelope and she retrieved a leather-bond journal.

"It's only an old diary." Eliza noted with disappointment.

Anais opened the aged cover to reveal the inscription within.

"It's Mother's diary. Don't you see? She must have recorded all her secrets. Why else would she hide it away?"

Eliza sat up with renewed enthusiasm. Her initial disappointment at not finding a copy of a birth certificate was all but forgotten and she anxiously wrung her hands as Anais read in silence.

"What does it say?"

"Be quiet, let me read." Anais scolded.

"Read it out loud." Eliza whined.

"I'm writing this journal in hopes that someone will find it someday and will know the suffering I endured at the hands of my mother. First let me say that I recently found a copy of my birth certificate and now know that I was adopted. I don't recognize the names of my real parents and will probably never know why they chose to give me up. I cry every night wondering what my life would have been like if they had only kept me.

I now understand why it is so easy for my adoptive mother to torture me so. I have always wondered why it was that my sister was spared while I was used so callously for what my mother insisted was the good of the coven. My sister is the true Lewis. I am nothing. I wonder if the coven is aware of my paternity or if they too have been fooled as I have these many years."

Anais stopped reading and wiped a tear from her eye.

Eliza looked at her sister curiously. "Don't stop." She insisted.

Once again Anais picked up the journal and cleared the lump from her throat.

"As far back as I can remember, my mother and her coven have used me as a sacrificial element. I was told it was an honor even as I lay bleeding on the floor. I was told I should be proud of the sacrifice I was making for the good of the coven, despite the pain I suffered. They have experimented with herbal concoctions, which they fed to me. They have poisoned my body and mind with images no child should see. I have been drained of so much blood I couldn't stand on my own and stripped of my dignity for mere sport. I will not rest until I see my mother and her coven pay for their crimes against me."

Both Anais and Eliza realized the hypocrisy of their mother's words. What she had accused their grandmother of she too had done to her own coven—her own daughters. Despite her hatred for her mother she had in essence become her.

"Do you think Father knew about all that?" Eliza asked.

"She had to have shared her hatred of her mother with him at some point. They had lived together in the very house where she was tortured. At some point he must have heard about the home's history, if not from her then by someone in the community."

Anais considered what she read for a moment. "I don't feel bad for her. She chose to repeat the sins of her mother instead of rising above them. If anything it makes her even more evil knowing the pain she's inflicting firsthand."

Eliza nodded, wondering if she too was destined to carry on the tradition. She also had used her name to inflict pain on others and had enjoyed watching them suffer. Perhaps she was more like her mother than she knew. Maybe the pain and misery she endured had been necessary for her to face the facts and break the cycle. In her self-reflection she was unaware that Anais had returned the journal to its hiding spot and was attempting to move the wardrobe on her own.

"Help me push this back." She called out.

"What about the journal?"

"I don't think we should read anymore. Some things are better off locked away. Besides, if I'm going to find a good hiding place where I can watch the ceremony, I need to get going."

Eliza agreed though she was intending on returning to finish reading the journal as soon as possible. It was imperative she knew what her mother experienced so she would be certain not to repeat their mistakes.

Anais made certain her younger sister was fed and safe in her room before leaving the house.

"I'll be back soon. Don't leave your room unless you have to use the bathroom and keep the doors locked. I'll use my key to get back in."

A worried look passed over Eliza's face.

"Don't worry...I'll be careful and I'll tell you everything when I get back."

Eliza nodded although she felt little relief. She watched from her bedroom window as her sister straddled her bicycle and took off, quickly disappearing from sight. She stood at the window long after the sun set, reflecting on everything they had learned. Although it was apparent Anais felt some sort of empathy toward their mother, she felt none. On the other hand, she found no joy in it either. Four years ago she might have celebrated at the news of her mother's pain, but the longer she waited for the day of reckoning, the greater the cost was to her soul. She couldn't even recall the last time she felt elation, just for the simplest pleasures in life.

Her mind drifted back once more to early memories of her father chasing her through the tall grass until she stumbled and fell to the ground. He would drop down beside her and tuck a dandelion behind her ear, brushing her wild hair away from her face. They would lie side by side on the old porch swing on hot summer nights listening to crickets chirp and suck on sour stalks of rhubarb they plucked from the garden until she eventually fell asleep. Those were the memories that kept her going when all hope seemed lost. Remembering the love of her father and feeling his love in return even after he passed had still somehow kept the darkness at bay.

Pulling down the shade, she looked around her room for something that might make her feel closer to her father, but there was nothing. Feeling the sudden urge to find something, anything of her father's she left the safety of her room.

Chapter Eleven

Anais reached the perimeter of the field just as the sun was setting. Using a downed elm tree as a point of reference, she quickly gathered its fallen branches to hide the bicycle's reflective surface. She could hear the distant mutterings of the covens as they made the long journey to the center of the field and she used their voices to guide her in their direction. Her heart pounded loudly in her ears, drowning out the sound of any creature that might be in her vicinity as she cautiously stepped one foot in front of the other in as straight a line as she could, hoping she would be able to find her way out again.

Although it wasn't hot, it was warm enough to bring out the mosquitoes and she fought the urge to slap her skin as they sunk their feelers into her flesh. Perspiration caused by her lengthy bike ride made its way down her back, creating a wet beacon to every flying insect in the field, inviting them to feast on the salty nectar. Somehow, nearly simultaneously as she stepped closer to the center of the field, the insects retreated as though there was an invisible wall blocking their entry.

Relieved that she wouldn't have to endure an evening of their endless torture, she took a settling breath. In front of her the tall grass had been hacked away in a circular shape. Inside the circle a pentagram had been carved into the ground, and a candle representing each elemental station was placed in its proper location. In the very center of the circle was a vessel to collect liquids.

Anais strained her eyes for a better look, but the ceremony was about to begin and the sisters along with their male counterparts had begun to assemble. Those members not participating in the coupling ritual acted as escorts, placing each couple at the appropriate post before retreating silently into the background.

When all the couples were positioned, Helena – along with the High Priest from the men's coven – entered the center of the circle. From out of the darkness, the remaining members of the sisterhood appeared, placing flower wreaths on the naked female's heads before signaling the group to join hands.

A nervous shiver ran down Anais's back as one of the sisters passed within six feet of where she knelt. When the opening chant began she used the opportunity to look around her for a safer, more suitable hiding place. Locating an unfriendly outcrop of thorny bushes to her left, she made a beeline for the spot, catching her pants leg in the process. Quickly she muffled her mouth to keep from screaming out as she pulled the thorns from her flesh. Now secure in the knowledge that no one would venture close enough to the bushes to discover her, she settled in to watch the ceremony.

Like their female counterparts, the warlocks were also naked, though their bodies were covered in tattoos. Each man appeared to represent one of the elements and the artwork branded on their bodies told a story similar to what she had seen in books. The most beautiful of all of them was the representative of Fire, whose body was painted in shades of red and orange. Upon his back was a forward-facing dragon, breathing flames in all directions. Its eyes appeared capable of piercing her very soul, even from a distance. Poker-hot daggers decorated his upper arms pointing down-ward in the direction of snakes that wrapped around his lower arms.

Anais wondered what image his chest might display and she silently prayed he would turn around so that she might admire his chiseled physique.

To his left stood the representative of Earth whose body was adorned with the image of a mountain range. Although she couldn't make out the finer details from where she was hiding, it was obvious even from a distance the tattoo had a great amount of elements. Like his brother, his arms were also adorned, though muted in comparison. Next to Earth was Water, represented by a young man not much older than her. It appeared as though his work was not quite done though his arms were decorated with beautiful blue water-falls.

At the top of the circle representing Spirit was possibly the oldest member of the men's coven. Upon his chest was a large dove in flight. His upper arms appeared to have images of rope, which wrapped around in the symbol of eternity. The final element, Air, was difficult to see from her location, though she assumed his artwork would include images of the sky.

Her fascination with the warlocks drowned out the low chanting of the group and she didn't realize they had stopped until she heard her mother's voice alone. One by one, she called each couple to the center of the circle where they lit their candle before returning to their places. When each of the couples were back in position, the chanting resumed. Anais repositioned herself for a better view, once again coming in contact with the painful thorns. This time she scratched her cheek and she immediately felt the warm flow of blood making its way down her face where it soaked the collar of her shirt. Unable to do anything about it for the moment, she returned her attention to the circle, where once again the couples appeared to be entering the center one at a time.

Now the High Priest held a dagger up to the heavens while chanting softly to himself. As each couple approached they offered their palms, which he sliced open before holding their hands over the vessel to collect a small amount of blood. As the couples returned to their spots, the watchers returned to bandage their wounds before once again disappearing into the darkness. When the process was complete, a combination of herbs was added to the blood before it was passed around the circle for all to consume. For what seemed an eternity, the group swayed in rhythm as somewhere in the distance a flute and bongo played. When it appeared the couples were no longer in control of their faculties, the watchers led them off into the tall grass.

Anais strained to see even one couple from where she hid, but the bushes blocked her view. Determined to witness a coupling, she ventured out, following the path the couple closest to her had headed. Before she saw them, she heard the distinct sound of a passionate kiss. Unsure whether or not she really wanted to witness their coupling now that she was so close, she hesitated.

Though to her it was just only an instant, it was long enough for her mother to observe the intrusion and she suddenly appeared out of no-where. Grabbing the startled girl by the arm, she dragged her to the circle, now occupied only by the watchers and the High Priest.

"It seems we have an intruder. She has witnessed that which is only to be seen by the eyes of our sister and brotherhood."

Anais trembled, fearful of her mother's wrath.

"I'm sorry...I"

"How dare you speak without permission to do so?"

Anais lowered her eyes to the ground. A sickness grew in her belly and she struggled to keep it down.

"Since she is the sinful consequence of my lust, I shall leave her punishment to you." Helena handed her frightened daughter over to the High Priest."

"So you would humiliate your respected mother for an opportunity to witness our sacred ritual?"

Anais hung her head, afraid to respond without proper direction.

"Perhaps it is that you wish to participate in the coupling yourself?" He suggested, raising her chin so that their eyes might meet.

Anais shook her head.

"How old are you, child?"

"Fifteen." Anais replied in a barely audible voice.

"It's a shame. You are much too young to experience such things. However…if watching is what you've broken our sacred gathering for, then watching is what you shall do."

Anais looked to her mother for protection, but she only saw her back as she walked away, allowing the High Priest to drag her off into the tall grass. Afraid to struggle, she permitted him to lead her, guided by the animalistic sounds of the coven members union. When they reached the edge of the prepared ground, the Priest placed his hands on her shoulders, preventing her from trying to move away.

Through the darkness she was unable to identify the individuals, though she was close enough to feel the heat of their passion. Despite her fear and shame, she found herself enchanted by the thrusting naked bodies before her. Her once trembling body relaxed as the couple that was seemingly unaware of her presence mesmerized her. Feeling the tension drain from her shoulders, the High Priest tightened his grip to remind her of her shame, but she refused to look away. Outraged by her attitude, he dragged her away from the couple and back to the circle.

"This child of yours challenges my good nature, Priestess. I suggest we teach her a lesson she won't soon forget."

Helena's face reddened with fury at her daughter's defiance.

"Do with her as you wish, she is no longer my daughter."

Anais starred at her mother's cold eyes and knew whatever was to come would be worse than anything she had previously endured.

As she watched in horror, a tall branch was driven deep into the ground. Seemingly without direction, the male and female watchers began weaving handfuls of sharp grass into a whip that resembled a cat of nine tails. Whether or not the possibility of an intruder had been discussed prior to the ceremony along with the punishment to be received, she didn't know, but the group appeared to work together in robotic fashion. By the time the torturous tool was completed, the couples were returning to the circle and were informed of her shameful crime.

Anais searched the crowd for her mother's face, hoping she might have a change of heart, but if she was there, she couldn't find her. Her former friend Sarah Walcott was selected to relieve her of her clothing. Anais silently pleaded with her peer, whimpering as her naked body was exposed for all to see. Next one of the male watchers was tasked with strapping her to the post exposing her on all sides and protecting only her spine. Her body shook as she sobbed, pleading with her captors. The High Priest raised his hand to silence her.

"You've come here knowingly in violation of that which you yourself have been a part. You are not an innocent wandering the fields. You came here with a purpose. You came to watch a sacred ritual intended only for those amongst us. For that, you must be punished."

Once more the brothers and sisters joined hands as they made a tight circle around her. None among them showed a sign of resistance as they took turns whipping her naked body with the sharp grass. When they were done her bruised and bloody body was removed from the post and the circle then turned their backs to her in a sign of rejection. Unable to stand, she collapsed on the ground where she continued to lie as the remnants of the ceremony were taken away and nothing remained but her broken spirit and darkness. Even the moon, previously full and bright, hid behind a thick cluster of clouds.

From a distance Helena watched in sadistic satisfaction as her once favorite daughter crawled toward the road on her hands and knees.

Chapter Twelve

Eliza cautiously made her way down the stairs; fearful her mother might have left a watcher behind to keep an eye on her daughters. Once she reached the first floor she made a precautionary check of its rooms to confirm that she was alone before retrieving her father's old flashlight from the junk drawer in the kitchen and heading out into the dark night.

Whether it was the light breeze blowing against the back of her neck or just the thrill of sneaking out of the house, she wasn't certain. All she knew was the icy chill that touched every nerve from the back of her neck to the top of her head was screaming for her attention, warning her to proceed with caution. She ran as fast as she could through the tall grass to the old shed, falling twice and scrapping both her knees and the palms of her hands. The flashlight took a beating as it flew from her hand and came crashing to the ground. The second time she fell, the light went out and she had to feel through the grass until she felt the cold metal. When she finally reached the shed, she breathed a sigh of relief.

There was something about crossing the threshold that made her feel like she was stepping back in time. Little had changed within the walls besides an inch or so of dust and half a dozen cobwebs. She wondered if she closed her eyes and thought really hard, her father might appear before her. It was silly, she knew, but she couldn't resist the urge or opportunity to see his face one more time. Turning her back to his workbench, she closed her eyes tightly, concentrating on the memory of his face. When she couldn't bear the wait any longer, she spun around and opened her eyes. Her eyes filled with tears.

"You're so *stupid*." She scolded herself.

Furious that her experiment had failed, she flew into an uncontrolled rage, tossing things about like a toddler throwing a temper tantrum.

"I hate you, I hate you, I hate you." She screamed; smashing mason jars filled with nuts and bolts against the back wall.

She reached for an old tin can and pulled her arm back to throw it when something across the room caught her eye. Grabbing the flashlight, she pointed it in the direction of the back wall where its light caught the reflection of something metal protruding from a hole she had made in the wall. Nearly making the width of the room in a single step she dove to the floor, oblivious to the countless sharp object including broken glass and nails scattered around her. To her amazement what she had uncovered was a hole in the wall that was disguised by an old beat-up seed sign. Inside the hole was a metal box about the size of a book. Carefully lifting it out of the wall, she examined each side before carrying it back to the workbench. Although there was a keyhole and the box was locked, she inserted a screwdriver into the hole and easily released the latch. Holding her hand atop the box to prevent it from opening before she was ready, she tried to prepare herself for more disappoint. What if it was empty? What if its contents held more questions than answers like the last one? Ultimately she decided she had nothing to lose and lifted her hand from the cover.

Inside were two letters, one addressed to Anais and the other to herself. If only Anais were with her now. Eliza struggled with the decision of whether or not she should open her letter or wait until her sister returned so that they might read them together. On the one hand, if she opened and read her letter now she could spare her sister the pain they were certain to experience should the letter contain bad news. On the other, if the letters contained the answers they were looking for, she would like to have someone to share the moment with. Yes, she decided, she had waited this long, she could certainly wait a couple more hours. No sooner had she made the decision then her eyes settled on the destruction she had caused. A wave of guilt and sadness washed over her.

"I'm sorry, Father. I didn't mean what I said. I'll come back tomorrow and clean up the mess."

She looked around, listening carefully as if she half expected to hear his voice assuring her that he loved her and accepting her apology. When she saw no sign of his presence, she placed the letters back in the box, grabbed the flashlight and headed back out across the field. After returning the flashlight to the drawer, she climbed the stairs and secured herself back in her room.

Anais was going to be upset with her for leaving her room after she had promised not to, but Eliza was certain that when she held her father's letter in her hand, all would be forgiven.

Noting the time, Eliza prepared for bed, hoping she would be able to stay awake until her sister returned. Not knowing just how long the ceremony would be and taking into account that her sister would have to ride her bike home, she settled in, anxiously clutching the two letters to her chest.

She wasn't certain what time it was or how long she'd been asleep, but she awoke to the sound of a slamming door and footsteps rushing up the stairs. Fearing the worst, she tucked the letters under her pillow and closed her eyes just as her door flung open. She could feel her mother's breath upon her cheek as she leaned in to make sure at least one of her children had obeyed her and stayed home. Satisfied she was fast asleep; she tiptoed out of her room, closing the door softly behind her.

Eliza took a deep breath and strained her eyes as if it was possible to see through the walls into her sister's room. Trembling, she prayed her sister had made it home and had not been spotted, though her mother's apparent rage said otherwise. Next door she could hear her mother muttering to herself as she ranted and tore apart her sister's room. Although a wall separated them, she could clearly make out the sounds of drawers being emptied and clothes being shredded.

Too afraid to venture out of her bed, Eliza clung to her covers for protection. The crushing lump in her throat was strangling her and she covered her mouth with her hands to release the sobs building up inside of her. Where was Anais? Was the coven holding her? Was her furious mother looking for something or just intent on destroying her sister's room out of anger? The only thing she knew for certain was something had gone terribly wrong and if she already wasn't, her sister would certainly suffer the consequences for whatever transgression their mother accused her of.

As quickly as the tirade began it was over and the only sound coming from the room next door was heavy controlled breathing as though her mother had simply put a pin in her anger with a plan to return to it later. Eliza focused her eyes on the shaft of light underneath her door, watching for her mother's shadow to pass before it. Despite her fear and a silent promise to her sister that she would stand beside her, exhaustion gave way to sleep.

In the darkness, Anais stumbled and dragged herself toward home using her bicycle as a crutch to support her. What had taken her less than thirty minutes on bike, took her nearly three hours of painful walking. Her prayers for a passing car that might stop and give her a lift were unanswered, making her question whether or not there even was a higher power looking out for her faithful followers as she had been told. It wasn't the first time she had questioned her mother's teachings and she struggled to consider the alternative. To be all alone in a world where mothers tortured daughters and women she'd known all her life turned their backs on her was simply too much to bear. The weight of all she had come to realize in the past weeks and months came crashing down on her and she crumbled to the ground, where she buried her face in the crook of her arms and wept. There were no walls here to muffle her pain and her cries were carried across the open fields. The night owl returned her cries with its own as if it too felt the loneliness of the darkness.

All the small creatures of the night that had kept her company as she made the long walk toward home, vanished in the wake of her misery; leaving only the crickets and a distant rumble of thunder. She lay on the road long after her tears had dried and the familiar sounds of the night had returned, comforted by their ability to face danger and return once more to life, as they knew it. Perhaps she too could return to some sort of normalcy if such a thing even existed in Wells.

When she finally reached the end of the long driveway leading up to her home, she was too tired to fear what might be inside. Slowly she inched her way up the hill, numb from the pain she had endured. A single light shone on the second floor of the house and it was in her room. She envisioned her mother waiting at the foot of her bed, arms crossed over her chest with a scowl on her face.

She wasn't prepared for the chaos she found. Inside, her once tidy room appeared as though a tornado had tore through, leaving only the walls standing. Her bed was stripped of its linens, which were shredded and tossed to the floor along with the contents of her bureau drawers. The few trinkets that adorned her bureau and nightstand were shattered into a million pieces, dotting the floor with shards of broken glass and porcelain.

Anais gingerly made her way to her bed, avoiding what she could and bearing the pain of whatever she couldn't. Certain that she would realize the full weight of it all in the morning; she lay atop her bare mattress and closed her eyes.

Every muscle in her body ached, while her bloodied flesh screamed from the mere touch of the old mattress against her open wounds. Her hair, damp from perspiration, clung to the back of her neck; making it difficult to turn her head from one side to another. Carefully she turned to her side and drew her legs up to the fetal position, grunting in pain as she did so. Any shame she felt earlier of her naked body was shadowed by her will to survive through the night. Although none of her wounds were life threatening, the sheer magnitude of all she had endured over the past hours was enough to make a grown person wish for death. She too had considered it briefly on the long journey home and had it not been for her little sister, she might have simply laid down in the middle of the road and waited for a passing car to crush the life from her lungs.

Eliza…she had nearly forgotten about Eliza. Certainly she had been witness to their mother's rampage. She only prayed her room was the only destruction she had caused. It wasn't beyond the realm of possibility that she might punish Eliza for her sister's sins. It wouldn't be the first time she had inflicted pain knowing that the recipient was innocent.

With as much intensity and determination as she could muster, Anais pulled herself from her bed and followed her earlier path to the door. She stopped at the threshold, listening for any kind of indication her mother might be lying in wait. When she was satisfied it was clear, she went to her sister's room, closing the door behind her. Afraid to turn on the light, she felt her way across the room until she came in contact with the foot of the bed. Only then did she brave turning on the bedside lamp to confirm her sister was well and fast asleep, but she wasn't prepared for what she saw.

Sitting on the edge of the bed, only an arm's reach away; she starred into her mother's evil eyes. Anais stumbled backward in shock, covering her mouth to suppress the scream that would surely wake her sleeping sister.

Helena said not a word before grabbing her eldest daughter by the arm and dragging her out of the door and down the hallway toward the stairs.

She said nothing as she yanked her down the stairs to the main floor of the house and again down the basement stairs where she stopped and pushed her onto the floor. Anais struggled to catch her breath, fighting back tears as her wrist came in contact with the hard floor and she felt the bone snap.

"How dare you?" Helena snarled through gritted teeth. "How dare you violate the sanctity of my coven? Did what you saw amuse you?"

Anais shook her head, afraid to speak.

"Once again my sisters have witnessed my humiliation by the actions of my own children. Have you no sense of loyalty?"

Helena paced the floor with her fists tightly clenched at her sides as Anais trembled with fear.

"I have given you both the power of the Lewis name and the strength to carry out the work of the coven and what have I gotten in return? Your betrayal! I expected as much from your sister. She is too strong and stubborn to be led. But you…I had hoped to mold you into a great leader, one that could carry on my work when I was too old to lead. I had hoped your recent setback was just that – a setback that in time would pass. I thought that you would do whatever you felt you needed to do and return to the fold."

No longer angry, Helena seemed to have drifted to a state of reflection, a calm before the storm if you will.

Anais cradled her broken wrist waiting for the moment to pass as it always did whenever her mother ran out of steam and needed some time to regroup. She wasn't prepared for what she saw when her mother turned around to face her once more. Tears stained her mother's cheeks and her bottom lip quivered as she struggled to regain composure.

"Why do my children hate me so?"

Was she supposed to answer? Anais was afraid to speak.

"Have I not given you everything you desire? Tell me what it is that I've done wrong."

"Nothing." Anais whispered.

"The truth…you owe me at least that much." Helena insisted.

"You care more about the coven than you do us. We could never live up to your standards, no matter how hard we tried. All we ever wanted was a mother that loved us."

Helena sat for a long moment in complete silence, considering her daughter's words.

"It's true that the coven is important to me, as it should be to you. Our future depends on the survival of the coven. Without it, we have nothing. What I do, I do for all of us, not just for myself. Perhaps you are still too young to understand. We are not rich; we depend on the coven for our continued existence. The little bit of money I make reading palms and preparing herbs is barely enough to see us through the cold winters. Maybe if your father was still with us I might have been allowed the luxury of spending time with you and your sister outside of the coven, but things didn't work out that way."

Anais listened, watching her mother closely for signs of building anger.

"The sisterhood is more than just a group of likeminded individuals, Anais. The sisterhood helps us in many ways. What I can't buy, the women provide. Whether it's the outgrown clothes of their children for you and your sister or home-made breads for your supper, the sisterhood looks out for us. These women come from some of the most powerful families in Wells. What they can offer goes far beyond anything I could provide to you on my own. We might not have the prettiest house in town or the nicest car, but the influence the coven holds over our community spreads well beyond the town's borders."

Anais waited, wondering when or if her mother would explain how abuse of her children as well as others, helped their cause. As if she were somehow telepathic, Helena's eyes fell to her daughter's cradled wrist.

"Does it hurt?"

Anais nodded, finally letting a tear slip down her cheek.

"I won't apologize for your suffering. Pain builds character, Anais. We gain strength through our own misery. Someday you will thank me for making you stronger."

"I think I need a doctor."

"You're probably right. Unfortunately, that isn't an option. It would raise too many questions for you to be seen in this way. Despite the fact that most of the community chooses to look the other way when it comes to coven business, they are not very tolerant when it comes to our old school methods. No...I will dress your wounds and set your wrist. You will stay home from school until you heal."

Cheryl Kennedy

Chapter Thirteen

Somehow Eliza had managed to sleep through her sister's return home and what laid in wait for her. Her sleep however, was not without its own suffering as she fought off demons she'd only seen in books and read about in her mother's journals. When she awoke the house was eerily quiet and she lay in bed an extra fifteen minutes, building up enough courage to check on her sister. Pulling on a robe, she listened at the door for sounds of activity below. By now her mother should be preparing breakfast and packing their lunches for school. She was considering whether or not to climb back into bed when she heard her mother call her from below.

"Eliza…are you awake?"

Opening the door, she made her way quickly to the staircase.

"Yes, Mother."

"Well hurry up and get dressed. You'll be late for school."

Eliza wanted to ask if Anais was already up, but the look on her mother's face told her not to ask questions.

"Yes, Mother."

Eliza ran back to her room, hesitating at her sister's closed door. As if she could read her thoughts, Helena called out once more.

"You don't have time to doddle, Eliza, get moving."

This time she didn't respond to her, instead making a beeline for her bedroom, where she grabbed the first pair of pants she could find and pulled a shirt from its hanger in the closet. Quickly dressing she grabbed a pair of socks and shoes and made her way downstairs to the kitchen.

Gobbling down her breakfast, she avoided making small talk, keeping her eyes on her cereal bowl. Likewise, Helena busied herself at the kitchen sink until she reached for the keys to the car.

"Are you ready?"

It wasn't really a question Eliza knew so she dropped her spoon into her bowl, tugged on her socks and shoes, leaving her laces undone and followed her mother out the door. Although the school was a short drive, the endless silence made the trip unbearable. Finally Eliza couldn't take it any longer.

"Is Anais sick?" She asked, trying to sound as nonchalant about the question as she could.

"You sister will be studying from home for the next couple of weeks. I'm certain she'd prefer to tell you why herself. You'd be wise to learn from your sister's mistakes, Eliza. It's really not necessary for history to repeat itself if we learn from it."

Eliza starred out the window, trying to decipher what her mother was trying to say, though she suspected she wouldn't fully understand until she was able to speak to Anais. It was going to be a long day. While she was somewhat relieved her sister was apparently well enough to speak and she would be allowed to spend time with her, she worried that seemingly, the extent of her injuries were so great that she was unable to attend school.

After dropping Eliza off at the middle school, Helena drove over to the high school and informed the front office that her daughter was suffering from pneumonia and wouldn't be able to attend classes for the next couple of weeks. The secretary promised to notify her teachers and see to it that her assignments were forwarded to her so that she could keep up with her studies. Satisfied, Helena returned home to keep an eye on her daughter in case she had any notions of running away from home.

Not that she was in any condition to do so.

Eliza spent the entire day staring at the clock in hopes that if she concentrated hard enough, she might be capable of speeding up time. The effort seemed to have the opposite effect, however, as the day dragged on endlessly. When the final bell rang, she was the first to jump out of her seat and make a mad dash for the door, leaving her teacher yelling at her back for her to slow down. Rather than waiting out in front of the school as she normally did to walk home with her friends, she took off running as fast as she could until her lungs felt like they were going to burst and she had to stop to catch her breath. Once more able to continue, she jogged at a slower pace until her house came into view. Even from a distance she could see that there were several cars in the driveway and once again she felt panic set it.

It was very unusual for the coven to meet so early in the day, so whatever the reason for this break in tradition, Eliza was certain it couldn't be good. If she had to venture a guess, it had something to do with Anais. She could only hope whatever punishment her sister had endured during the previous night was to be the end of it. But, as she approached the house, she recognized the scent of lavender and jasmine wafting through the sitting room's open window. Eliza was familiar enough with the practice to know the combination had something to do with love spells. In her mind, that was an indication that whatever had happened the previous night was over and her mother had moved on to business as usual.

Confident it was safe to enter, Eliza made her way up the porch steps to the front door. The sound of joyful laughter and excited chatter filled the sitting room as she approached. As a rule, she was neither allowed to interrupt, nor partake in any coven business, but the blissful spirit of the women drew her in and she had crossed the threshold before she knew what she was doing.

Undisturbed by her presence, the women continued to laugh and talk without hesitation.

"Tell us Sarah…was it everything you thought it would be?"

Sarah's normally pale face reddened in her obvious discomfort.

"Don't tell us you're shy now, dear, we couldn't help but hear your cries of pleasure last night."

Sarah lifted her head, looking at the faces of her sisters, who were all eagerly awaiting her response. Eliza too inched forward into the circle; curious though not quite sure she understood the question. Sarah opened her mouth to speak and a ripple of excitement filled the air only to be quashed as their leader pointed a finger in her daughter's direction.

"It would appear my eldest daughter is not the only one to violate our sacred coven. Let us adjourn so that I might remind her of her place."

One of the sisters who Eliza recognized but didn't know by name stepped forward.

"Please, Helena. Clearly she meant no harm, she's just a child."

Helena glared at her subordinate. "A child that should know better than to enter our sacred circle uninvited."

"Let us forgive her lapse in judgment in the spirit of last night's successful union."

"Perhaps you too need to be reminded of your place, sister." Helena threatened.

Eliza shrank back as her mother pushed forward, locking eyes with her disobedient child and grabbing her hard just above the elbow.

"Would anyone else care to tell me how to raise my child?"

Silence and fear replaced the previously euphoric coven. Only Eliza could be heard quietly whimpering as her mother's strong grip tightened in anger.

"I will not stand in judgment by any of my inferiors. I am the leader of this coven and the sole parent to my children. It falls upon me…only me, to see that they show proper respect. If any of you are uncomfortable with my methods of discipline then perhaps you should look elsewhere for your spiritual guidance. Greatness and weakness do not coexist. One must be set aside for the other to prevail. Only with a strong hand can we expect to achieve true greatness. I will accept nothing less of my coven or my children."

The sisters nodded mutely, keeping their eyes on the floor as if they feared meeting their leader's gaze would mean death or something worse: eternal damnation.

"If we're all in agreement then, tell me, sister," Helena directed her question to her outspoken subordinate, "what punishment is it she deserves?"

"That of your choosing." She replied, barely loud enough to be heard.

"And if I should choose to whip her like her sister?"

"We stand behind your decision."

"Do you see, Eliza? Do you see how quickly they turn against you to save themselves? See how they turn a blind eye when it suits them? These are your teachers, your shopkeepers, your librarian… these are our community's trusted leaders. These are the women who your friends look up to, who hide their true selves behind masks of altruism. They are merely puppets content only to do my bidding. They have no more respect for you then they do themselves."

"That's enough."

In unison the circle turned to see Anais, now battered and bruised, standing at the threshold.

"How dare you?" Helena spat.

"What, Mother? I have nothing left to fear. Do your best and when you're done…what then? You'll sit back on your throne of self-righteousness and condemn those that have the audacity to pity me. I'm not a child anymore. The only person here deserving pity is you. You have no love in your heart. We are all merely tools to be used and tossed aside when we no longer have any value to you. God forbid anyone question your motives or the path you lead them down."

Helena's grip tightened on her daughter's arm as she struggled to reclaim control over the room.

"You have no idea what you're talking about, Anais. What I do, I do is for the coven, not myself. I am nothing without them. A priestess is only as good as her weakest member. Our strength comes in numbers. Perhaps my methods are old school, but adversity builds character…it makes us strong. We have amongst us the result of many generations of carefully crafted breeding. We have a fourth generation alchemist, the first daughter of a direct descendent of Giles Corey. John Proctor's blood runs through the veins of our most trusted watcher and I have only begun to scratch the surface. Our ancestors spent decades if not centuries refining the bloodline. Our generation may be the closest we will ever come to perfection."

Helena let go of her daughter's arm to stand alone. "I have been preparing for this role for my entire life. I have sacrificed more than any of you will ever know to lead this coven. I have watched some of my closest allies turn their backs on me simply because they didn't have the stomachs to do what was necessary."

"Necessary, Mother? Was it necessary to have your own flesh beaten within an inch of her life and left to claw her way home? Was it also necessary to pit your children against each other to see who came out on top? Was it necessary to shame young girls for the satisfaction of others? Tell me, Mother…was all that necessary?"

"I will not stand here and be judged by you or anyone else. It should be enough that I say it is. I should have earned at least that much respect. I will not have you question my motives. Everything I do…EVERYTHING, will lead this coven to greatness."

The coven's youngest member then stepped forward, kneeling before their leader to show her respect.

"Perhaps if we understood exactly what it is we will do that will bring us this recognition, it would be easier to accept. I have only the utmost respect, Priestess, but I do admit to questioning whether or not it will all be worth what I've given up in the end. I am extremely grateful for your confidence in me and the opportunities that being a member of the sisterhood has given me, but it has come with a great deal of sacrifice on my part."

"As well it should, Sarah. As I said before, we must suffer before we can rejoice. As for the moment of greatness, the one event that Wiccan sisters will read about for generations to come…that I cannot answer. I can only tell you what I myself know. My vision told me of a child born within the coven. It is through this child that history is made. That is all I know. The fact that the Goddess has enlightened me with this great vision should be enough to secure your trust in my leadership. The elements bind us together as one. Our brothers share my vision and so they were willing to share their seed. They have not asked for anything in return."

"But what if our coupling does result in this child of your vision? Will the father wish to claim the child as his own? Wouldn't he have as much right to the child as we do?"

"Let me worry about that. Now, the most important thing is that we come together as a group. Don't let my ungrateful children sway you. They are the product of their father's unrelenting delusions. He didn't share my visions for our future and so he took every opportunity he could to challenge me in front of them. Perhaps I was foolish to believe that in time they would come to realize it was me, not him who had their best interests in mind."

Anais grabbed her sister by the arm, as if she meant to challenge her mother.

"Go ahead, Anais…run away and take your ungrateful sister with you. Neither one of you is worthy to stand in my presence."

"Helena! I beg you, stop this now before you fracture your family beyond repair."

Helena turned to face her outspoken sister, expecting her to bow her head or retreat in fear, but she stood her ground.

"So it's a challenge you want? I will not step down as the leader of this coven. Whether it's a coven of twelve or a coven of one, I will lead until I take my last breath. And if any of you wish to challenge me for the seat, I encourage you to speak now."

Silence spread throughout the room as the women looked into each other's eyes, as if by doing so they could hear each other's thoughts. The air was thick with tension as seconds turned to minutes and still no one spoke. Amused by their sudden quiet, Helena drew back her shoulders and stood a little straighter; confident the matter was settled. Then from the back of the room a voice was heard.

"I challenge you." Everyone turned in unison as Eliza stepped forward, breaking her sister's grasp. "I challenge you for your seat."

Helena laughed. "You? You are a child, not to mention the fact that you're not a member of this coven."

Eliza looked around the room, but no one else was laughing.

"I've been studying hard. I might need help, but I think I would be a good leader."

"Have you heard enough of this nonsense? A child cannot lead a coven."

The outspoken sister stepped forward once more.

"She's right, Eliza. It takes years of practice before you could be considered for the position. I know your intentions are good and someday I'm sure you'll lead a coven of your own, but now is not your time."

Eliza lowered her head, defeated before she'd even begun the battle.

Helena rested her hand on her shoulder as a sign of dominance.

"We are getting off track. We are so close to greatness I can taste it. We mustn't allow ourselves to veer off course. I will be the first to admit my temper sometimes gets the better of me, but all of my intentions have always stayed true. Whether we stay the course together as a united front or I go it alone, is up to you. Either way my vision was clear, our power lies in a child not yet born to this world; a child that bears the mark of the pentacle. It's not clear what power she will hold, supernatural or otherwise, but it is through her that we bind the elements to form the most powerful force this world has ever known. Our ancestors will rejoice from beyond the grave at what we have accomplished."

Too weak to stand any longer, or perhaps deflated by the turning of the tide of emotions, Anais slowly made her way back upstairs without even her sister realizing she had gone. From the safety of her bed she listened to the excited murmuring of the sisterhood as they discussed the ramifications such a powerful being might have on the world. As far as she was concerned, the entire vision was a fabrication designed out of necessity to hold a crumbling empire together. The fact that the sisters were so willing to believe her only proved her dominance over them. The longer she listened, the more she pitied the group of misfits who not so long ago were her peers. Now she wondered how it was her mother managed to rein them in for so long. Even at her impressionable age, she still had the ability to see through the deception. How was it that the others could not?

A knock at the door interrupted her thoughts and she looked up just in time to see her sister stick her head in the room.

"Can I come in?"

"Of course."

Anais waited for her younger sister to cross the room and plop down on the end of her bed before speaking.

"That was very brave of you to stand up to Mother like that. Stupid, but brave."

Eliza smiled broadly.

"It sounds like things are status quo down there. It amazes me how quickly they forget."

Eliza shrugged pulling two envelopes out of her sweater.

"What's that?" Anais inquired.

"I found them in the wall of the shed last night." Eliza held her hand up to stop whatever scolding her sister was about to give. "They're from Father. I didn't want to open mine until we were together...you know, in case it says something bad."

Anais nodded, relieving her sister of the envelope marked with her name.

"I think we should wait until we're alone. It's too risky to open them with so many people in the house."

Eliza sighed, disappointed but agreeing they would open them together when the time was right. Whenever that might be.

Chapter Fourteen

The girls spent a restless night, each holding onto their father's letters as if their lives depended on it. When morning finally came, Eliza entrusted her sister with her letter before heading off to school. Fearful of her mother's wrath, she got dressed quickly and made her way downstairs; where her mother had breakfast waiting for her.

"Good morning, Eliza."

"Good morning, Mother."

Helena eyed her daughter, sensing her fear.

"I know you and your sister aren't fond of me these days. I only hope that someday you'll understand why I do the things I do. Don't think for a moment I don't love you."

Eliza looked deeply into her mother's eyes, searching for even a twinkle of compassion, but all she saw was darkness.

"I was thinking you might enjoy helping us prepare for the summer solstice. I know it's quite a while off, but there's so much to do we could use an extra set of hands."

"But I'm not a part of the coven."

"Not yet, but if you work hard and regain the trust of the sisterhood, perhaps there may be a place for you in the future."

Eliza considered her mother's words. After everything she had witnessed she was no longer certain she wanted anything to do with the sisterhood. Each time she had given her mother the benefit of the doubt she had been hurt.

"You don't have to decide right away. Think it over. The coven won't meet again until next week."

Eliza nodded, grateful for once her mother understood her hesitation.

When she arrived at school the halls were buzzing with speculation regarding what had taken place at the Lewis house the previous afternoon

Immediately she was surrounded by her own small coven who bombarded her with questions, allowing her very little time to answer. Curious onlookers stood close by hoping to hear whatever tidbit of information they could get to fuel the gossip. Eliza pulled her group aside, hoping to contain it.

"I don't know what you heard, but it was nothing out of the ordinary. Just a regular meeting."

"I heard your mother went crazy."

Eliza laughed. "She's always been crazy, that's nothing new."

"I heard no one's seen Anais in days and that your mother did something to her."

"I don't know where you're getting your information from, but Anais is at home. She's sick is all. It has nothing to do with my mother."

Disappointed, the group broke off into pairs leaving Eliza standing alone in a hallway full of disapproving faces that were eager to condemn her and everything she stood for. She could feel the color rise in her cheeks as her peers whispered amongst themselves and she was torn between wanting to scream or run away and cry. Ultimately the bell rang and the crowd dispersed, leaving her shaken but grateful she didn't have to make the choice.

When the final bell rang, signifying the end of the school day, Eliza quickly bolted for the door, hoping to disappear before anyone had a chance to corner her. As luck would have it, a fight broke out on the playground and all eyes were focused there, allowing her to slip away undetected. Running as fast as she could to distance herself from anyone that might attempt to catch up with her for more questioning, she made it home in record time.

She had expected her mother to be waiting at the door, but instead she was quietly tending to her herb garden, looking content. Eliza hesitated, wondering if she should interrupt her to say hello. Above, Anais tapped her finger on the windowsill to get her sister's attention. When she didn't respond, seemingly lost in thought, she tapped harder. Eliza looked up and saw that her sister was motioning her inside. Glancing once more in their mother's direction, she opened the door and ran up the stairs. Anais met her at the door.

"I thought you'd never get home…quick, let's open our letters before she comes inside."

"What if she catches us?" Eliza wasn't willing to risk another explosion like yesterday.

"We'll sit at the window so we can keep an eye on her. Come on."

Anais grabbed her sister by the arm and dragged her across the room just as quickly as her injured body would allow her.

"You go first." Anais insisted.

"You're the oldest, you should go first."

Anais shook her head and pressed Eliza's letter into her hand. Eliza swallowed nervously, taking a deep breath to prepare herself. With trembling hands, she opened the sealed envelope and read aloud.

"My dearest Elly...If you're reading this letter I can only assume I am no longer with you. I have hidden it in a place only someone with your determination would find. I hope that you are old enough to understand what I am about to tell you and know above all else that I love you more than anything in the world."

"By now you will have come to realize that Helena is not well. Her life has been consumed by her quest for power. Only after we fell in love and decided to marry did she find out she was not a Lewis. Her family had kept it a secret as long as they could, but could keep it no longer when her birth certificate was required for our marriage license. I wish you had known her then, before her name and everything it stood for was ripped away.

Before that she was like a delicate flower, compassionate and nurturing. Despite everything she had endured as a child, she believed that everyone had goodness inside of them, just waiting to come out. I had hoped that eventually she would come to trust again, but it wasn't to be. Instead, hatred destroyed her. She was resentful of everything she didn't have and blamed everyone but herself.

"A distance grew between us that couldn't be bridged. I reached out to her sister, the real Lewis, for help and I found in her what I was missing with Helena. I won't apologize for the love that we shared; I have never regretted it for a

moment. I am, however sorry that because of my actions, you have suffered the consequences. It wasn't until she became pregnant that Helena suspected we were involved and by then it was too late. You were already growing in her belly. I suspect the complications with the pregnancy were the result of some vile concoction brewed up by Helena, though I was never able to prove it. Your mother died moments after you were born.

"When I refused to give you away, Helena had no choice but to accept you as her own. I should have known that it was a mistake and I should have taken you away, but I couldn't leave dear Anais alone with an uncaring mother. I had to stay to protect you both. Things only got worse. She pitted you against each other, favoring your sister. She controlled everyone that mattered in this town. It would have been impossible for me to gain custody and so I tried to protect you as best as I could.

"I have become quite ill and I believe whatever poison killed your mother is also killing me. I don't share Helena's belief in spells and curses and know that herbs and chemicals are the real sources of her magic. I've seen what she can do by mixing one with another and she's only getting better at it. If I should die, know that it is by her hand, but do not confront her with that knowledge. If she suspects you know her secret, I fear what she might do. Instead, just prepare yourself by

studying her family's grimoire, which she hides behind a secret panel in her closet. Everything she knows, she learned from there.

"My only regret is that you never got the chance to meet your true mother or feel her love as I did. Anais is your only family now. Don't let Helena tear you apart...Your Loving Father."

Eliza stared down at the tear-stained letter, only looking up when her sister covered her hand with her own.

"I'm so sorry, Eliza. It's terrible that you had to find out this way."

"She's not my mother."

Anais waited, expecting more to come, but Eliza simply stared at the letter in silence.

"Would you like to go for a walk? You know...just to get out of the house and clear your head?"

"You should read yours."

Anais shook her head. "It can wait...come on, we'll take our bikes down to the beach."

Eliza nodded, though she wasn't certain what good it would do. Helena wasn't her mother. Her true mother was dead. She would never hear her voice or feel her embrace.

Anais led her sister by the hand, taking soft steps toward the staircase and down to the main floor of the house. They reached the front door just as Helena entered through the kitchen.

"Wait here. I'll tell Mother…I'll tell her we're going out for a bit."

Eliza stood motionless, neither eager to leave or wishing to stay. Anais returned before she had time to form a simple thought in her head, as though she was in a time bubble. Once again, Anais took her by the hand and pulled her out the door.

"I thought she said you couldn't leave the house until you were healed?"

"After what happened yesterday, she wouldn't dare deny me time with you."

"Are you able to ride?" Eliza asked, very concerned over her sister's battered appearance.

Anais nodded, settling onto her bicycle seat and motioning for Eliza to lead the way. They rode together slowly in silence, Anais because of her injures and Eliza simply because she was in no hurry.

"Do you want to talk about it?"

"I don't care that Helena's not my mother. I'm actually happy about that. I'm just sad that I'll never get to know my real mother. I don't even know what she looks like."

"There has to be pictures around somewhere. I'll help you look for them. I know it's not the same as meeting her, but at least you'll have something to hold if you want to talk to her."

"Talk to her?" Eliza stopped pedaling and hopped off her bike.

Anais had to turn around and come back to her.

"Whenever I'm sad and I want to talk to Father, I take out a picture I have of him and talk softly to him. It makes me feel like he's still here. It probably sounds silly but it helps."

"No, it doesn't sound silly. Do you think that Father was right? That she poisoned her, I mean."

"I used to think there was no way Mother had anything to do with Father's death. I honestly believed he died from pneumonia or something like that, but that was before I saw who she really is. You were right all along, Eliza. I'm only sorry it took me so long to realize it."

"It makes so much more sense now. I have always thought she loved you more because you are so much prettier than me."

"Oh Eliza…I hate it when you say stuff like that. I've always seen your beauty even when you were certain there was none to see. Clearly Mother intended to make you feel bad about yourself by pitting us against each other as Father said. You've always been strong-willed and I'm sure she thought that bringing me into the coven and keeping you out would surely make you lose your confidence."

Eliza was suddenly ashamed of all the mean things she had done to her sister over the years, not to mention her evil thoughts. Anais sensed Eliza's regrets and reassured her.

"Whatever happened in the past, we need to put behind us. Wipe the slate clean, as they say. From now on it's you and me together…sisters to the end."

By the time the girls returned to the house, dinner was waiting for them on the table, with a note from Helena stating that she had stepped out and would be back before bedtime. Both Anais and Eliza were grateful that they would be able to enjoy their dinner without her dissecting every word that might come out of their mouths. At least now, they could chat freely without the fear of revealing the secret they had uncovered.

Eliza stabbed a large chunk of meatloaf, then examining it closely.

"You don't think she'd poison us, do you?"

Anais looked at her plate apprehensively. "I don't think so. She may have gotten away with it once, even twice, but if anything were to happen to us; I don't think even the sisterhood would be able to protect her."

Satisfied, Eliza stuffed the meatloaf into her mouth and followed it up with a scoop of mashed potatoes. While they ate, they considered what secrets if any might be in Anais' still unopened letter. Their recent search of the entire house had produced little in the way of family history. At the time, Anais thought it odd, seeing that so many generations had resided within the walls of the dilapidated home, but it was now clear Helena had rid the premises of anything related to her childhood.

"Father's letter said there's no such thing as spells and curses. Do you believe that?" Eliza asked.

"I suppose it depends on the beliefs of the person being cursed. If someone believes in such things they can be convinced whatever happens is magic. It's really about the power of suggestion and how the brain works."

"So it is real?"

"In a way. yes. It's hard to explain."

Eliza considered her own experiences and wondered whether or not even Helena had the power to control her mind. She liked to think she was actually much stronger than those who had fallen victim to the High Priestess, though she admitted her hatred toward her mother obstructed rational thoughts and fears.

Anais knew whatever her sister was thinking couldn't be good, so she attempted to distract her. "Why don't we clean up the dishes and go up to my room? I have some new nail polish we can try out."

Eliza nodded, although her mind was clearly elsewhere. They quickly cleared the table and washed and dried the dishes before making their way upstairs.

Chapter Fifteen

Out at an old forgotten cemetery, neglected and hidden from view by tall grasses, Helena and several members of the coven placed lavender, cinnamon and wormwood on hot coals atop the grave of one of the town's founding fathers. Beside Helena, on either side, stood her most trusted watchers, ringing bells to summon the dead. Covered head to toe in a black robe, Helena spoke in soft, luring tones.

> *"Blood of our fathers, from whence we came,*
> *We summon you now to put out this flame.*
> *Through the portal of time our arms we extend,*
> *As we form this bond that has no end.*
> *Only through blood do we find what we seek,*
> *For without your aid our power is weak."*

With the tip of the ceremonial blade, they each pierced the palm of their hands and watched as the blood dripped down onto the hot coals.

Joining hands to pass each other's blood from sister to sister, they swayed in rhythm to the hissing coals until nothing was left but ash. Her underlings dutifully waited for direction as to what to do next.

"The tide is turning, sisters. There are many who seek to break our bond. We have become too strong and they fear us. If we stand together, committed to our craft, there is nothing they can do to break us."

Somewhere in the darkness a small voice spoke out. "Who is it that looks to harm us, Priestess?"

"They have no face; they hide behind false praise among us. They seek to discredit me and all that I stand for. They turn sister against sister, looking for cracks in our armor. We mustn't let fear or harsh tongues distract us from our mission." Helena turned and walked away, signifying the end of the gathering.

Her confused subordinates followed suit.

Distracted by all of the recent events, Helena instinctively drove the short distance back home, stopping at the foot of the long drive to stare up at the old homestead. Nothing about it brought back fond memories, though she desperately tried to find even a glimmer of tenderness from her childhood. It was no wonder her marriage had failed when she had no memories of her parents showing one another any kind of affection. In her mind's eye she saw only grim faces, hardened by years of misery. Like their ancestors before them, they had chosen a path of isolation, segregated from the masses, capitalizing on the community's fears. Never once had she considered accepting her adoption and distancing herself from the Lewis clan. Instead she dug in her heels, doing whatever was necessary to keep her secret and with it her power.

As she climbed the creaking staircase to the second floor, she could hear her daughters chatting and smell the toxic fumes of nail polish. Seeming to be unaware of her arrival, the girls gossiped shamelessly while Helena stood outside Anais' bedroom door, hidden from view. When the topic, as it always did; reverted to the coven, Helena made her presence known.

"Don't you girls have anything better to do than to gossip?"

"Sorry, Mother…we were just wondering whether or not any of the women were showing signs of pregnancy." Anais attempted to sound casual, despite her rapidly beating heart.

"It's much too early to tell. Now it's time the two of you get ready for bed."

Eliza obediently slid off her sister's bed, careful not to touch the bedding with her still damp fingernails.

"Good night, Mother."

"Good night, Eliza." Helena then eyed her daughter curiously. There was something in the way she said "Mother" that hinted toward some hidden meaning. Certain it was a shot at her lack of parental aptitude; she made a mental note of it and let it slide. She was far too exhausted to get into another battle of wits so soon after the last one. Despite her expertise in the area, she always preferred to initiate the battles, not be provoked into them, as seemed to be the way things were going lately. The last thing she wanted was to let Eliza think she had any kind of control over her situation.

Once alone, Anais reached under her pillow and withdrew the envelope containing her father's letter. Although she had promised Eliza they would read it together, she feared the contents might be for her eyes only. Perhaps it would be better if she read it first while she was alone, she thought. She listened to be certain both her mother and Eliza were settled into their beds before gently sliding a fingernail along the sealed envelope. She would have to reseal it later so that Eliza wouldn't know she had read it without her. A shiver ran down her spine as she pulled the folded letter from the envelope and she tucked the blanket tighter around her to calm her nerves. Placing the letter inside a book, in case someone entered the room unexpectedly, she began to read.

"My lovely Ana, your beauty pales to the kindness in your heart. While others see only the face of loveliness, I know that you possess gifts far beyond your beauty. I am certain your sister has shared the secrets written within the pages of my letter and I pray you don't think less of me for what I have done. You and your sister are my pride and joy and there is nothing I wouldn't do or sacrifice for you. Over the years I have watched your mother pit you against your sister despite my protests. I am too weak to do what needs to be done, but you and Eliza together can do what I was unable to. Protect each other from harm. When the time is right, stand before her as a united front. Only together can you break the hold she has over you and her coven. I only hope that you have found these letters before it's too late.

Remember always, the love that I hold for you and your sister. That love will live on well after I am gone. Your loving Father."

Anais carefully folded the letter and placed it back in its envelope, resealing it as best she could before placing it back under her pillow.

Turning off her bedside lamp, she laid her head down and softly cried herself to sleep.

In her room down the hall, Helena meticulously noted every detail regarding the coupling ritual in her personal journal, leaving out her daughter's embarrassing intrusion. She hoped that in years to come, historians would look to her journals as a source of reference, proving her significance to the Wiccan world. Looking over her entry, she smiled, confident she had performed the ceremony exactly as it should have been. She had no doubt Sarah would bear the blessed child, making her placement of her to her second in command that much more insightful.

The vision had been as big as a surprise to her as it was to her coven. Never had she had such clarity before. It was as if she was watching a movie play out before her and she was the only audience to the performance. Though the mother's face was unclear, the hands that held the child were those of a young woman. No calluses or veins spoiled the smooth skin that gently stroked the brow of the newborn child. Only Sarah, who was practically a child herself, fit the description. Making her second in command was a logical choice. Once the child was born it would prove she had greater insight than any of them imagined and they would fall at her feet begging her forgiveness for their past doubts.

Helena absolutely refused to consider what would happen if no child was born as a result of the coupling ceremony. The vision had been clear. If only her own daughter had been old enough to participate in the ritual. The satisfaction of having her own flesh and blood bear the chosen one would have been the seal of approval from the Goddess herself. Helena shrugged. It was of no matter. She had been chosen as the vessel through which the vision was delivered and that fact alone carried a lot of weight. Now she had only to see it through and make certain the mother was well cared for and that no harm came to the fetus.

It had been nearly two decades since she last referred to the family grimoire's vast inventory of spells and she hesitated to utilize it now. At one time it had been her sole source of reference in teaching herself the old school ways of the many past generations, but when she realized her true lineage lay outside the Lewis clan, she tucked it away, vowing to never use it again. Now however, she feared the stakes were much too high to risk not using it, so she stepped into her closet's hidden chamber to retrieve the book.

The closet's secret chamber had been built during the original construction of the home for the same purpose it continued to be used. Fearing the community's intolerance of witchcraft, the Lewis family hid the instruments of their trade from prying eyes. It had also been used as a hiding place on more than one occasion when members of the family were hunted for crimes against their neighbors. The shelves had been constructed more recently when Helena had sought to organize the contents of the room to make it more efficient. The plywood door replaced a small sliding panel, barely big enough to crawl through.

As she entered the room now, as she often did in preparation for ceremonies, everything appeared as it should be. It wasn't until she couldn't locate the family grimoire that she finally realized someone other than herself was aware of the room's existence. Scanning the shelves to see what else might be missing, she noted the absence of a particular set of bones and knew immediately who was responsible for violating the sanctity of her private chamber. Helena tried to recall the last time she had seen the remains of Little Boy Blue, placed on the shelf so many years before. She should have known Eliza wouldn't give up until she found the pet she loved so much, but what about the family grimoire? How long had she studied the pages written by her ancestors? While her hatred had never wavered for her unfaithful husband and sister, her feelings for Eliza were less clear. Although she was a constant reminder of betrayal, she acknowledged it was beyond her control. Eliza was as innocent a victim as she was. Still, it was all she could do to raise the girl, whom she often butted heads with. Unlike Anais, who was easily manipulated into doing whatever was asked of her, Eliza was stubborn and defiant. The fact that she was the spitting image of her late sister only contributed to her contempt for the child. If Eliza was now privy to her ancestor's extensive knowledge, there was no telling what she was capable of.

Crawling out of the confined space, Helena perched herself on the edge of her bed as she contemplated what to do next. If she confronted Eliza she would most certainly deny any knowledge of the book's whereabouts and she would likely never see it again. On the other hand, the longer Eliza held the book in her possession, the more knowledge that she would gain. Helena's only option was to watch the girl closely in hopes she might reveal the book's location inadvertently.

Chapter Sixteen

Several months passed during which time Helena resurrected her coven, once again bringing new members in to replace those that had fallen out of grace. Breathing new life into the sisterhood consumed her, giving her little time to keep a close eye on the girls. Although she continued to hope Eliza might reveal the location of the grimoire, it was no longer a priority.

Anais had taken a part-time job in her attempt to save money for college, which was only a year away and Eliza busied herself with her own coven. The thought of living alone with Helena when Anais went off to college terrified her. With Anais, she had a buffer – someone to stop her from acting on impulse – which was a good thing.

Although the coven kept Helena away from home and preoccupied, whenever something didn't go her way she directed her anger at the girls, rather than risk upsetting the sisterhood. When that happened, Anais would just remind her sister that it wasn't her fault and whatever Helena said in anger was the result of her own insecurities and had nothing whatsoever to do with Eliza.

The weeks after the coupling ceremony had been the worst. Helena had bet everything on a successful outcome and while she waited for some sign of confirmation, no one was immune to her mood swings. Only Sarah had become pregnant as a result of the coupling, but had miscarried a few weeks later. When the phone call came, not even Eliza was prepared for the effect it had on Helena. She tore through the house with no thought for the suffering mother, who had just lost her child.

The girls barricaded themselves underneath the basement staircase. Sandwiched between moldy boxes of strange relics belonging to their previous generations and old wooden crates containing mason jars filled with herbs, they held onto each other.

Like a tornado, Helena tore through the house; toppling furniture and smashing dishes; letting some stand untouched while others were destroyed, all the while screaming and swearing at the top of her lungs.

Anais attempted to shield Eliza's ears from the worst of it, but failed miserably. The obscene vulgarities spewed from Helena's mouth with sickening precision, leaving nothing off limits and little to the imagination.

Not one of her coven sisters was exempt from insult and it seemed there was no limit to how low she would go. Her tantrum dragged on so long she finally lost her voice. This only infuriated her more and she stormed through the house in search of a victim to take her anger out on.

When she heard her mother climb the stairs to the upper floor, Anais made her move.

"Run…go out the bulkhead and run as fast as you can. Go get Theona and bring her back here."

Eliza resisted. "What about you? What if she finds you?"

"Don't worry about me. I can defend myself. Now go and hurry."

Eliza ran, tripping over boxes and stopping to right them, while Anais motioned for her to leave them and get out. The distinctive squeak of the bulkhead alerted Helena to their hiding spot and she took to the stairs two at a time, anxious to catch them in the act of escape.

When she finally reached the door to the basement, Anais was waiting for her at the bottom of the stairs, blocking her view and path to the bulkhead.

"How dare you to hide from me?" She managed to whisper through strained vocal cords.

"You have to stop, Mother. You've scared poor Eliza half to death."

Helena descended the stairs, stopping at the next to the last step so that she stared down at her eldest daughter. Anais searched her eyes for any sign of coherence, but she was wild with rage.

"Eliza has gone for help. Someone will be here soon."

Once again Helena attempted to speak. "Don't you dare threaten me. I gave you life and I can just as easily take it away."

Anais mustered up as much courage as she was able.

"You're not right, Mother. There's something wrong with you. You need help."

As soon as she had said it, she realized her mistake and she looked behind her for an escape route. She only turned for a second, but that was all it took for Helena to overpower her. Helena grabbed her by the shoulders and pushed her to the hard concrete floor. There was a sickening thud as the back of her head came in contact with the floor and she immediately lost consciousness.

Helena stood over her daughter's motionless form, unmoved by emotion. Something inside her had snapped. She felt no attachment to the figure before her. It was as if she were watching a movie play out in front of her with no investment in the characters. While a small pool of blood formed around Anais's head, Helena climbed back up the stairs, entered the kitchen and poured herself a cup of coffee.

Eliza, with Theona—the oldest member of the coven—entered the house cautiously, listening for signs of Helena's whereabouts. All was quiet but for the distant sound of humming coming from the kitchen. As they made their approach, it soon became obvious that something wasn't right.

"Helena?" questioned Theona. "Is everything okay?"

Helena smiled at her guest before returning her attention to the coffee in front of her. Eliza clutched the woman's hand.

"Eliza, why don't you go find your sister while I have a chat with your mother?"

Eliza nodded, grateful to leave the room. Preoccupied with Helena's strange behavior, she searched the entire main floor of the house before heading upstairs to her sister's room. When she didn't find her there she started to panic and ran quickly down the stairs in the direction of the basement. She was halfway down the basement stairs when she saw her sister lying motionless below and screamed for help. Running to Anais's side, she laid her head upon her sister's chest to listen for a heartbeat. Although her breathing was shallow, she was still alive and Eliza quickly pulled off her sweater to wrap around her sister's bleeding head.

Theona gently moved Eliza aside to examine Anais. "We need to get her to the hospital. Run upstairs and call for an ambulance."

"But what about Mother?"

"Don't worry, she's in no state to harm you or anyone else."

Eliza quickly obeyed, taking the stairs as quickly as possible. It took the ambulance nearly ten minutes to arrive and Eliza paced the porch anxiously waiting while Helena sat quietly sipping her coffee. The police arrived shortly after the ambulance, speaking at length with Theona before calling for a second rescue to transport Helena as well.

"Can I ride in the ambulance with Anais? She'll want to see me when she wakes up." Eliza begged.

"She's not going to wake up for a while, Sweetie. We're going to follow the policeman back to the station so we can tell him just what happened."

Eliza glanced at the officer, who gave her a reassuring smile.

"What about Mother?"

"She's going to the hospital too. We'll check in on them later."

Eliza nodded, even though she wasn't really convinced that a hospital was the right place for Helena. If it were up to her, she would lock her up and throw away the key. Whatever happened to

Anais, Helena was responsible and Eliza would make sure everyone knew it. She might look like a scared fourteen year old, but on the inside she was much stronger than anyone knew.

At the police station, Eliza anxiously paced the floor while Theona followed a detective into another room. The police officer who responded to the call approached her with a can of soda and a bag of potato chips.

"I thought you might like something to eat."

Eliza smiled, accepting the food and then following the officer to a waiting area with chairs, tables and a stack of old magazines.

"Why don't you have a seat here for a little bit. I'll be back in a few minutes to get you."

Eliza nodded, grateful to be off her feet after her long run to Theona's house. She ate her snack slowly and thumbed through a couple magazines before the officer returned for her.

It was nearly six o'clock by the time they finished up at the station, each having given their statement; and Theona suggested they stop to get a bite to eat before checking in on Anais. As they drove the short distance between the police station and the restaurant, Theona couldn't help but notice Eliza's far off gaze. Despite the fact she had known the girl all her life; she had spent little time with her away from her mother's prying eyes. This was the opportunity she had been waiting for to find out what was really going on behind closed doors.

"How are you doing over there?" She asked, placing her hand on Eliza's knee.

Eliza shrugged. "Okay, I guess."

"Do you want to talk about it?"

Eliza stared back out the window. "Do you think they'll lock her up in one of those places for crazy people?"

"I don't know, Sweetie. It's now up to the doctors. There's nothing the coven can do for her. I suppose they'll run some tests, keep her in the hospital until she comes around, then decide what to do from there."

Eliza nodded. "I hope she never comes home."

The coldness with which she spoke sent chills up the watcher's spine. There had been rumors of course, how could there not be, but they were just that. No one really knew what went on inside the Lewis house. Theona remembered when Helena's mother had run things. Not unlike her daughter, she had used the power of her name to control, not only the coven, but the leaders of the community as well. The fear of doing battle with a great witch, if she in fact was one, kept everyone in line.

When Helena had taken over, there was an attempt to finally regain control of their seats, but they quickly found out she would stop at nothing to get her way. Helena's knowledge of herbal potions gave her the upper hand. Because many of the herbs disappeared quickly from the system, no one was able to prove she was responsible for the deaths of several local farmers' livestock as well as a flu-like epidemic that spread throughout the community. Her motivation had come when the local farmers banded together to put a stop to their fields being used for coven rituals.

A town meeting had been held and there a representative from the farming community had addressed the matter in an open forum. Not only did the coven clear large sections of the fields without permission, but their bonfires had caused one family to lose its entire crop. Their spirited ceremonies frightened the cattle and more than once a chicken or two had been stolen and then scarified; their carcasses left mutilated and drained of their blood. The council had no choice but to enforce an old town ordinance banning open flames without a permit from the town. Fences were erected where there previously were none and dark roads were lit by newly installed street lamps.

The cost to the town was significant enough that budgets had to be modified and several people lost their jobs.

Eliza barely spoke a word as the waitress filled their water glasses and Theona placed their order. When the waitress was out of earshot, she continued her questioning.

"How long have things been bad at the house?"

Eliza shrugged her shoulders. She still wasn't sure she could trust the woman. What if she told Helena what she said?

"It's okay, Sweetie, you can talk to me. I know you're afraid."

Eliza met her eyes and saw only kindness.

"As long as I can remember. I think she had something to do with my father's death."

"The sisters think so too. You're not alone. For a long time now there's been talk of an over-throw, but no one has been willing to step up to the plate. In the last few years we've lost nearly half our members and it's taken its toll on those that stayed. When she announced her vision there was hope things could change for the better. If the vision was real and a child was born to one of our sisters, then the power would be shifted away from your mother."

"Do you believe the vision was real?" Eliza had been struggling with that question for months. "She never had visions before."

"We couldn't be sure. On the one hand it seemed to come at the very critical moment when she was losing control of the coven. Anyway, the announcement seemed a convenient way to bring the focus back to her. On the other hand, a child born from a vision who would lead us to greatness was simply too good to ignore. We had to take a chance that it was real."

The food arrived and Eliza once again fell into silent thought, pushing her food around her plate, but eating very little. When it was clear she needed prompting, Theona spoke once more.

"The night of the coupling ritual was the final straw. Your sister was very lucky to have survived. We all met secretly for several nights afterwards to strategize. We decided it was in our best interest to do nothing until we knew whether or not a child was conceived. When nothing happened and Helena grew agitated, Sarah agreed to play the part of the chosen host. We knew we couldn't keep the ruse up forever; we just needed enough time to figure out our next move. We all agreed we would leave the sisterhood together as a united front. There was supposed to be a meeting tomorrow night. We decided to tell her in advance that Sarah lost the baby so that she had time to consider her next move."

"So she was never really pregnant?"

"No, none of us were. Don't you see, Eliza? She has no real powers, only the odd ability to convince others she does. Once it was evident her vision was merely another gimmick designed to control us, we realized we had nothing to fear."

"But what about all the people she made sick? Weren't you afraid she would come after you?"

"Not if she thought we were all simply disheartened by the failure of the coupling rite and collectively decided we didn't want to be involved any longer."

Eliza considered everything she said. Even at her young age it didn't make sense. There was no way her mother would accept that they had all decided to turn their backs on everything they believed in. "It would have never worked," she announced. "She would have known you were up to something. She said herself that you're all just puppets acting out her wishes. She would know you were conspiring against her."

"Perhaps, but it was a risk we were willing to take. We could no longer turn a blind eye to the suffering she was causing. If we stood together against her, she would be at our mercy, not the other way around."

Eliza rubbed her head; the day had taken a toll on her. Theona motioned for the check and she gathered her things.

"Why don't we stop off at the hospital to check in on Anais, then you can spend the night at my house?"

Eliza was too exhausted to argue; besides, the thought of spending the night alone in the old Lewis house was terrifying.

Chapter Seventeen

Helena remained in a catatonic state as the nurses removed her clothing and redressed her in a hospital gown. Leather straps secured her arms and legs to the hospital bed as added security for the protection of the staff. After an initial exam in the Emergency Room she was wheeled up to the psychiatric ward. An armed police officer stood at the door ready to alert detectives as soon as she was able to speak.

Helena quietly observed everything going on around her as though she was looking through someone else's eyes. She was unclear why she was witness to the situation and although she saw the nurse's lips moving, the ringing in her ears prevented her from hearing what she was saying. The nurse waved her hand in front of her face for no apparent reason other than to distract her from the armed guard at the door. He stared at her as if he knew something she didn't and she wanted nothing more than to ask him just what was happening, but she couldn't find her voice. An IV needle was inserted into her hand and she drifted off to sleep.

Two floors below, her daughter, Anais, remained unconscious while a CAT scan was performed to determine if she had swelling of the brain. A portion of her hair had been shaved so that the cut on the back of her head could be sutured and bandaged. Eliza and Theona waited nervously, just outside the room, for the doctor to inform them of her condition. Eliza stared blankly at the TV screen playing an episode of a court-room drama she cared nothing about, while Theona paced the floor. It was nearly eight o'clock when the doctor finally appeared.

"Are you here for Ms. Lewis?"

"Yes, I'm a friend of the family and this is her sister. How is she?"

"She's resting comfortably. She has a mild concussion and we're going to keep her overnight for observation, but she should be able to go home tomorrow."

Theona squeezed Eliza's hand and smiled.

"That's wonderful news. Can we see her?"

"She resting now, but if you leave your name and number at the nurse's station, we'll give you a call in the morning when she's ready to go."

Theona thanked the doctor and followed him out to the nurse's station with Eliza at her heels. She considered asking about Helena's status, but decided Eliza had worried enough for one day. Whatever her mother might be going through paled in comparison to what her daughters had experienced.

She had held nothing back when she gave her statement to the police. Whether Helena spent the rest of her life in a mental institution or behind bars was of little consequence to her at this point. The girls deserved better and whether she had to stand before a panel of physicians or in front of a judge, she didn't care, but there was no way she was ever going to allow Helena to regain custody of her daughters.

Early the next morning they returned to the hospital and were met by a pair of detectives outside Anais' room.

"We're here to take her statement, but we thought we'd wait until she had family here. The doctor has cleared her to speak with us. I promise we'll keep it brief."

Theona agreed but couldn't stop Eliza from rushing past them to her sister's side. Theona held the detectives back.

"Let's give them a moment, please."

"Of course." The older detective motioned for the younger one to step away from the door to give them privacy.

The girls embraced and exchanged gratitude that they were both okay before Eliza motioned for the others to enter. Anais relayed, as best she could, the events of the previous day up until the point her mother came down the basement stairs. After that, she said, she had no recollection of what happened, although she assumed her mother had caused her injuries.

"Where is she?" Anais asked nervously, looking past the detectives.

"She's under a doctor's care. You have nothing to worry about. She's not going to hurt you anymore." The older detective turned to Theona once more. "I think we have everything we need. You can take her home now."

After a brief meeting with a county case-worker to determine if the girls were comfortable accepting Theona as their temporary guardian, Theona signed the release forms and escorted the girls back to her house where she made them an early lunch of soup and sandwiches. Since she lived alone, the girls were given her guest room, which had a queen-sized bed, to share. Although she ate well, Anais was still very groggy from the medication the nurses had given her the night be-

fore so she made her way up to the room with
Eliza following close behind.

"I'll lay down with you just in case you need
anything."

Anais smiled, grateful to have Eliza by her
side.

Eliza kept a watchful eye over her big sister;
cautiously optimistic the worst was behind them.
Before long, with the comfort of her sister beside
her, she too fell asleep.

While the two girls slept, Theona phoned
several members of the coven to inform them of
the situation and suggest they hold an emergency
meeting. It was nearly three o'clock when the girls
finally descended the stairs, looking rested and
well and chatting like they didn't have a care in
the world.

"You two look a lot better. How are you
feeling, Anais?"

"Much better, thank you. Have you heard
anything about Mother's condition?"

"Not yet but I don't want you to worry about
it. I was thinking we'd take a drive over to the
house so that you girls can pick up a few things."

They both agreed and returned to their
conversation as they made their way out to the car.
It wasn't until they pulled into the long driveway
that they stopped talking and Theona immediately
sensed their apprehension. Glancing in the rear-

view mirror, she could see their weary eyes staring at the house on the hill.

"If you'd rather not go in you can just tell me what you need and I can get it for you." Theona suggested.

"No…it's okay." Anais replied. "We'll all go in together. It's just a house…nothing more."

Theona felt a twinge of guilt realizing she should have said or done something sooner. She suspected the girls were being abused and she had done nothing about it, putting her own fears ahead of them. If either one of them had lost their lives, she would have never been able to forgive herself.

"I'm so sorry for everything you girls have been through. I promise you, from here on out, I will do whatever I can to prevent her from ever seeing you again."

It seemed like too little to Theona, but the girls assured her the entire blame fell squarely on Helena's shoulders and no one else's. No one could have known what was going on inside that house and they didn't expect anyone to risk becoming the recipient of Helena's wrath on a hunch. Whatever happened in the past, Anais assured her, was in the past and they would only look forward.

The girls quickly gathered enough things to last them a week, while Theona waited at the threshold. Despite everything that had happened, she still respected the fact that it was not her home. Eliza finished packing first and joined Anais in her room.

"I packed as much as I could fit in my overnight bag." She announced. "Are you ready?"

"Almost." Anais replied, reaching under her pillow. "You should bring Father's letter just in case we don't come back."

Eliza nodded, hurrying back to her room to retrieve it.

Downstairs Theona could hear footsteps running back and forth. "Do you girls need help?"

"No, we're all set." Anais announced as she made her way down the stairs with Eliza close behind.

"Are you sure you have everything you need; toothbrushes, hairbrushes and all that?"

"Yes, Ma'am." Anais confirmed.

"Okay then, what do you say we go out for a bite to eat before we settle in for the night?"

The girls eagerly agreed. It wasn't often they got to go out to eat.

Theona had arranged for the other members of the coven to meet at her house later that same evening, once the girls had settled in for the night. Considering everything Anais had already been through, she didn't want her to have to face those that witnessed or had a hand in her whipping at the coupling ceremony.

Wells was a close-knit community and word traveled fast. As soon as the threesome entered the restaurant, Theona regretted her decision to take them out. All eyes focused on the girls as they slowly made their way to a table in the back of the restaurant. Even the waitress seemed to be most uncomfortable interacting with the teenagers.

Whispered voices didn't stop them from hearing their mother's name on their wagging tongues and then their faces turned red with embarrassment. Anais buried her face behind her menu, while Eliza stared right at the offenders through their disapproving eyes as if to challenge them. Most looked away, returning their focus on their meals, while others seemed angered by her defiance. Their expectation that she should cower down to their scrutiny baffled Eliza. She had done nothing wrong, so why should she feel ashamed?

"Ignore them, Eliza. They're just trying to get a reaction out of you. It's best for you to take the higher road." Theona advised.

"What do they expect me to do, cast a spell on them? Act like a lunatic? I don't even know these people."

"People tend to be curious about things they don't understand. They probably heard Helena had a mental breakdown and they want to see how the two of you are affected by it. The best thing to do is ignore them and they'll get bored and leave you alone. If you respond it will only make things worse."

Anais remained silent, peeking over the top of her menu occasionally. She found the whole situation humiliating. School was going to be a nightmare. By the time the waitress returned with their drinks, they had all lost their appetites, so Theona ordered a round of appetizers and called it a day.

On the way back to Theona's house, they stopped at the local video rental shop where she allowed the girls to select a few movies to take their minds off dinner. By the time they returned home it was nearly seven o'clock.

"Why don't you girls run upstairs and put your pajamas on while I make you some popcorn. I'll roll the TV cart from my room into yours so that you can watch your movies in bed."

The two girls smiled broadly, tugging at Theona's heartstrings. Once again she wondered exactly how bad things must have been that such a simple gesture could make them so happy.

Eliza raced up the stairs with Anais quickly following behind, while Theona collected herself and made her way into the kitchen. By nine o'clock the credits were rolling on the first video and the girls were fast asleep.

Downstairs the women of the coven were gathered quietly around the dining room table, eager for an update. Only those who had young children at home hadn't come for the emergency meeting. Theona poured coffee from a carafe while the women settled in.

"I know this is highly unusual, but under the circumstance I just didn't know what else to do. Obviously the time has come to replace Helena with a new appointment. I realize Sarah is next in line, but I think we'd all agree she's far too young for the challenge."

They all nodded agreement, including Sarah.

"Is there anyone here that would like to be considered for appointment?"

"What about Anais?" Sarah suggested. "I realize she's not a member of the coven, but don't you think we owe it to her after what happened at the field?"

"I know your intentions are good, Sarah, but Anais has no desire to join the coven, let alone lead it. Besides, she'll be going off to college next year. No, I think it's important we really think this through thoroughly and don't rush to make a rash decision. Helena isn't going anywhere. As far as I know, she still hasn't said a word."

The women spoke at length, debating the pros and cons of looking outside the coven, even considering bringing back into the coven some of the old members that had left their circle because of Helena's erratic behavior. They were all united on one thing and that was there would be a complete transformation of the coven's mission. They agreed fear had no place in the worship of their Goddess. Theirs would be a coven of peace and healing. Rather than rule the community with an iron fist they would invite them in to celebrate with them.

The seasons would be a time of celebration once again and the town would prosper as a result. No man, woman or child would have to fear their presence amongst them and no form of dark magic would be tolerated.

By the time the women left there was a new and renewed spirit between them and they each closely embraced one another and then sang each other's praises. It was decided they would meet again the following week, with each sister having accepted a task.

Chapter Eighteen

Weeks passed and the girls remained under the watchful eye of Theona. The court had granted her temporary custody when Helena was moved to the state mental hospital. With no improvement in sight, the judge suggested she consider a more permanent arrangement, at least for Eliza, who was under eighteen.

The girls quickly and easily settled into their new routine, grateful for the stability. While Anais focused on her studies, Eliza snuck off to meet with her own coven, which had all but deserted her during recent events.

At first she was disappointed that they hadn't rallied around her, offering their support or perhaps something to do to take her mind off things, but as the weeks rapidly went by, her disappointment only made her more determined than ever to prove to them her worth. When she called the first meeting they stared at her like she was speaking another language. It wasn't that they didn't know what to say, although they generally let her do most of the talking. No, it had more to do with the fact she called the meeting in the first place.

"What's the matter with all of you? Have you all lost your tongues since the last time we met?"

A chorus of apologizes filled the boxcar that was now their permanent meeting spot.

"Well then, speak up. I can't lead a coven of mutes."

"It's just that we're surprised you still want to do this…you know…because of what happened to your mother."

"First of all, Helena's not my mother. My real mother's dead. Second, now more than ever before we have an opportunity to do something big."

The girls stared at their leader with open mouths. Again Eliza reminded them they had voices and that they ought to use them. She then immediately regretted her words. What did she mean Helena wasn't her mother? Who was her mother? How did she find this out? Who else knew? Were all the rumors about Helena true? Eliza held up her hands to silence the girls before answering one question at a time. The girls seemed particularly interested in hearing about the rumored coupling ceremony, the details of which had been greatly distorted.

"I doubt most of that's true. I wasn't even there and Anais doesn't like to talk about it."

That didn't stop the girls from asking though and Eliza finally had to just make things up to get them off the subject. Seemingly satisfied with her answers, the girls settled back down. Eliza took firm control once more, passing out a handful of harmless spells for them to try out. Each piece of paper listed the purpose of the spell, the necessary ingredients, and the expected outcome. There were healings spells, protection spells, love spells and even a couple of money spells amongst the lot. Some of the girls had wanted to trade, but Eliza insisted they keep the spell they were given.

"You'll each get a chance to try them all, I promise. We're going to keep a journal of all successes and failures to see who has the most potential."

The meeting was cut short by a couple of teenagers in the mood for some privacy. The old Eliza would have stood her ground and insisted they find another place to make out, but if she had learned anything from Helena's abrupt break from reality, it was to pick and choose her battles and not expect to win them all.

Helena's fatal mistake was the assumption that she would always get her way. When things didn't go exactly as planned, she couldn't handle the disappointment.

Eliza wouldn't repeat history. She herself had plenty of time to make mistakes and learn from them. As the only surviving Lewis, she had no one else to fear. Instead, she graciously allowed the young couple entry, holding the sliding door open as each member of her coven descended the steps.

The following week, Eliza's coven met once again in the old boxcar to discuss their spell's successes and failures.

"Why don't we start with you, Misty? You were given a protection spell. Tell us what you did and whether or not it worked."

Misty stood up and nervously addressed the coven.

"The spell required a box that could lock, black glass, a sprig of pine needles and a piece of paper. I used my jewelry box for the spell and I painted the mirrors inside the jewelry box black. I didn't need any protection so I wasn't sure what to do, but then my brother came home crying and said one of the boys in his class wanted to fight him the next day after school, so I wrote my brother's name on the paper and put it inside the box."

"What happened?" Eliza pressed.

"He came home with a black eye." Misty lowered her eyes, embarrassed to face her leader. When it appeared she was about to cry, Eliza moved on to the next member.

"Morgan what spell did you have?"

Morgan quickly stood, anxious to reveal her successful outcome.

"I had a healing spell. It required a sprig of rosemary, some rose oil and pure water. I had some really bad cramps so I did the spell on myself. First I dipped the rosemary into the oil and drew the sign of the pentacle on my belly, and then I drank the water and buried the rosemary outside. A half an hour later the cramps were gone."

One by one the remaining members of the coven stood and revealed the results of their spells. Although most were failures, the successful ones were proof that the Book of Shadows was a reliable source of magic.

Eliza collected the spells and redistributed them, making sure everyone received a new spell. Although it normally would fall on the maiden to keep a record of such things, Eliza accepted the responsibility herself. It wasn't that she didn't trust anyone else to keep an accurate account; she was more concerned that the journal might fall into the wrong hands and their secrets would be exposed.

Theona allowed Anais and Eliza freedom to come and go as they pleased within reason and as long as they completed their chores and home-work.

Eliza took full advantage of her good nature, making trips out to the old house at least once a week to pick herbs from Helena's garden to use for spells. The coven relied on her to provide what they needed and she didn't want to disappoint. As long as she didn't have to go inside the house, she was comfortable enough to make the journey on her own.

Whenever time permitted it, she would visit her father's shed, finding comfort with his things. On those occasions she spoke out loud as if he were there with her. Sometimes she even waited for a response, hopeful that one day she would hear his voice again. She tried to convince Anais to join her on one of her trips, but her sister really wanted nothing to do with the old house.

"I know eventually we'll have to go back there to get our things, but until then I'd rather not. I don't understand why you like that old shed so much. It gives me the creeps."

Eliza shrugged; she'd explain if she could, but she wasn't really certain herself. All she knew was she felt her father's presence there, the smell of grease from the old car parts, the magazines with the pages folded as if he meant to revisit them someday; all the unfinished projects waiting for him to finish. Somehow it made her feel like he would be back someday. If there was a grave she could visit she probably would, but in its absence this was all she had. Even if the old house burned to the ground she would still have this reminder of him and of the short time they had together.

Theona watched from her bay window as Eliza made her way across the street. That girl was up to something, of that she had no doubt; but what it was she wasn't sure.

Anais seemed to have adjusted to life without Helena quite well. Not only was she excelling in school, making up the work she had missed when she was out, but she had been accepted into at least a half dozen colleges despite the fact she had missed many of the school's deadlines. Theona had encouraged her to go out with her friends more, but the once sociable senior seemed content to stay at home.

Eliza was a peculiar girl. Whether it was her constant state of dishevelment or the way she always seemed to be stuck in her own head, Theona wasn't certain, but whatever it was it gave her pause. She seemed a bit off and that concerned Theona greatly. It wasn't that she feared she might follow her mother's path, after all, she had shown her sister a great deal of empathy following their mother's attack. No, it was something else...

something about the way she sneaked around, always seeming to be on a mission of some sort. Theona had considered following her on more than one occasion, but ultimately she decided to trust the budding teenager and hope that in doing so, she would build her trust as well.

The girl's caseworker had provided her with a list of therapists in the area, should either of the girls show signs of stress, but Theona feared the suggestion of a counselor might make them feel like something was wrong with them, so she decided to take it day by day.

Rather than greet her caregiver when she entered the house like her sister always did, Eliza made a beeline for the bedroom calling out that she was home.

By the time Theona made her way to the staircase from the kitchen, she had already closed the door behind her. Once more she considered bringing her in for counseling just to set her own mind to rest, but she feared Eliza would resent her for it, so she quickly dismissed the idea. Perhaps it was actually better to simply provide her with a comfortable home and hope in time she would find interests more in line with other girls her age.

Eliza breathed a sigh of relief when she saw she had the room to herself. The only time she got to be alone lately was when her sister was off at the library studying, or at work. Once she was certain Theona hadn't followed her up the stairs, she reached under the mattress for the Lewis Book of Shadows. By now she practically knew the book by heart, she had studied it so long, yet each time she opened its cover she got the same feeling of excitement, as if she were seeing it for the first time. The massive manuscript smelt of days long ago.

Eliza wondered if it had ever seen the light of day or if it had always been hidden away in secrecy. Each page told a story all its own, marked with the remnants of past spells. An ashy fingerprint, a spot of oil, a drop of candle wax and even a smear of blood, told the story of her ancestors. She felt their presence through the pages as if they were there with her.

Perhaps it was because of the warmth in between the mattress and box spring or simply the fact she had opened it so many times, whatever the reason, this time when she lifted the cover the brittle leather broke free from the pages exposing the binding and something hidden within it. Eliza stared at the parchment for several seconds, too afraid to touch it for what it might hold. Finally, with a shaky hand she softly peeled the delicate document away from the book's spine. Rolled tightly and tied with a silk ribbon, the parchment appeared very old. Gently she pulled on the ribbon and unrolled the paper. The writing was done with quill and ink and was extremely difficult to read. Eliza took a deep breath and concentrated.

"Today I have condemned our very own Reverend George Burroughs to possible death. We must travel to Salem, where he will be tried with the others accused of practicing Witchcraft. Only our coven knows the lies that I speak, for it is with their instruction that I do so. Whatever shall happen will change our little town forever and the Lewis name will never be forgotten. I am torn between feelings of love for my former guardian and my loyalty to the sisterhood. I only pray that future generations will know the sacrifice I have made and will respect me for what I have done, for if there indeed is a heaven and a hell, I shall certainly reside in the latter."
Mercy Lewis

Eliza stared at the parchment, as if by doing so she might better understand the words on the page. Had this confession eased the conscience of her ancestor? Despite Helena's constant reminders that the Lewis name was significant enough to be mentioned in history books, she had revealed little of their ancestor's role in the Salem Witch Trials. It would seem from Mercy's confession that their role was less than honorable. Eliza wondered whether it was Mercy herself who placed the note in the binding of the grimoire or someone else.

Although she understood that there was a lesson to be learned from her family's past mistakes, she still didn't know what that lesson was.

Placing the fragile parchment into an empty bowl, she quickly struck a match and burned the confession. Confessions were a sign of weakness as far as Eliza was concerned. Right or wrong she had always stood behind her actions and she felt nothing but disgust for this young woman's regrets.

For all she had been through, Eliza was anything but weak. She wore her actions as a badge of courage. Even in her failures, she found pride in the knowledge that she had made the attempt. Yes, she was responsible for making girls cry, but hadn't that made them stronger? Yes, she had said some ugly things when provoked, but hadn't they deserved the harsh words?

She refused to apologize for other people's shortcomings. Despite her clarity on the subject she failed to see how similar her actions were to those of Helena. While Anais distanced herself from everything related to Helena and the coven, Eliza only dug in deeper. Where Helena had failed she would succeed, of that she was certain. Eliza was a Lewis, Helena was not and that would make all the difference in the world.

Placing the grimoire once again beneath the mattress, Eliza set to work making a list of goals she wished to achieve over the next several months. On top of that list was the acquisition of Mercy's personal journals. She had seen them years earlier when she was rummaging through the attic, but she had been far too young to read them or realize their importance though she thought enough to hide them away, deep in her mother's secret closet. Her recollection was that there were at least a dozen, if not more, hand-written journals. Of course it was possible they contained nothing of significance, but Eliza was betting on the fact they held more than one secret not found in the family grimoire. The challenge was going to be figuring out a way to get over there without arousing the suspicions of Theona. The last thing she wanted was her guardian asking questions. With both the grimoire and the journals in her possession, she would be more powerful than all her ancestors combined.

What her ancestors didn't have access to in the past was now readily available and the fact that Helena hadn't noticed the absence of the book in all the years Eliza had it in her possession told her one very important thing. Helena had never attempted the spells her ancestors wanted to but couldn't.

At dinner that night she tested the waters. "I was wondering if maybe I could stop by the old house after school tomorrow to get a few things."

"If you'd like to make a list I can pick them up for you?" Theona suggested.

Eliza moved her food around on her plate in an attempt to seem casual.

"It would probably be easier if I just go myself since I know where everything is."

"I don't like the idea of you going over there alone, Eliza. Maybe we can go together on the weekend."

Eliza wanted to protest but she didn't want to arouse suspicions. Instead she simply nodded her head and returned her attention to her dinner.

"Now that you mention it," Anais chimed in, "I'd like to go as well. We still have a ton of stuff in our bedrooms we should go through. Why don't the two of us go together? We can pack up everything we want to take and then you can pick us up when you get out of work."

"That's a great idea. Are you girls sure you'll be okay there by yourselves?"

The girls nodded, reassuring their guardian they would be fine.

The following day dragged by while Eliza fixated on the clock. The only thing she had thought about all day was getting her hands on the journals and time seemed to be standing still. When the bell finally rang, announcing the end of the school day, she was the first out of her seat and through the door. Despite calls from several of her

classmates, not to mention angry teachers screaming at her to slow down, she ran full steam through
the hallways to the school's main door. Outside
she looked up and down the streets for Anais, who
had promised to be waiting for her under the lone
elm tree, but she was nowhere in sight. Furious,
Eliza yelled out her name, hopeful the mere sound
of it would make her suddenly appear, but all she
saw was a sea of recently released students. She
stood like a statue on the steps of the schoolhouse
until no one else remained, each moment growing
more and more furious. How could she leave her
standing here when she knew how important this
mission was to her? She had already filled Anais
in the night before on her plan to retrieve Mercy's
journals. While Anais didn't share her enthusiasm,
she understood their importance to Eliza. What
possible reason could she have for standing her
up? Nearly half an hour had passed when she
finally set out on her own, determined not to wait
any longer. If Anais did come, she would know
where to find her. It didn't matter that she didn't
have a key. It wouldn't be the first time she had
snuck into the house.

First walking briskly and then running as
fast as her legs could take her, she was nearly
halfway up the drive before her lungs could take
no more and she had to stop to catch her breath.

While she tried to slow her breathing, she
looked up at the dilapidated house on the hill and

wondered what it would have looked like in its early days, when the paint was new and windows clean. She envisioned ladies in long dresses sipping tea from pretty cups while their children laughed and played. She reflected on her own childhood where such things were so obviously lacking. Certainly there must have been moments when she and her sister had laughed and played, though she couldn't recall any now.

She remembered how happy she had been when she spent nights at her friend Celeste's house. How she envied her friend whose mother was so kind and generous. Memories of the past refueled her and she continued on her journey up the long drive to the house.

After reports of Helena's breakdown and subsequent hospitalization spread throughout the community, the house had become a magnet for every wayward teenager in town. Nearly every window had been taken out by bricks and rocks, some wrapped in messages of obscenity – laced condemnation for every unfortunate event that had ever struck the town. Helena was blamed for every stillborn child, accidental death and every burned building, as well as financial losses. As things escalated and local police could no longer contain the violence, the windows were boarded up and "NO TRESPASSING" signs were posted at every corner of the property. A patrol unit was assigned to sit at the bottom of the driveway each night in hopes of deterring trespassers.

When she reached the front door she tried the knob more out of habit than expecting it to open. When it turned without resistance she thought perhaps Anais had been confused and thought they were meeting there rather than the school. Once more angry for having waiting so long for nothing, Eliza called out her name.

"Anais…Anais are you here? You were supposed to meet me at the school."

Hearing movement upstairs she headed up. The sound seemed to be coming from the end of the hallway where her own bedroom was located so she headed in that direction. She hesitated at the closed door, fearful of memories from the past. Once again she heard the sound of something heavy being dragged across the floor, only now it sounded like it was coming from the attic. Something inside her stirred and the hairs on the back of her neck stood up. She considered whether or not she should simply head back down stairs and out the door. Perhaps an intruder had made his way into the house and was going through their things. She listened more closely to the footsteps above. Clearly they were too light to be that of a man.

"Anais…Anais is that you?"

There was a brief silence in response, then followed by the thump of something heavy being dropped to the floor. Suddenly she wasn't feeling so brave. If Anais was trying to scare her, she wouldn't give her the satisfaction of knowing she succeeded, she would simply ignore her.

Opening the door to her room, she stepped inside. A layer of dust coated every surface of the shabby room and the air was stale and dry. She made her way over to her nightstand, and switched on her portable radio to drown out the sounds from above. Taking a quick survey of the room's contents she realized just how little she had. She hadn't given it much thought until they moved into Theona's house, but as she looked at it now she realized how void the room was of anything personal. Unlike Theona's rooms that were filled with knickknacks and mementos from the past, her own room contained only the essentials. Unless it served a useful purpose, like the tiny silver cup that held her hairpins, Helena had found such things unnecessary. Even the bedding had been the same for as long as she could remember and even then it had been worn. Although she had already emptied her drawers, she checked them once again to make sure she hadn't left anything behind.

Under her bed she found a stack of old books she had hidden away from prying eyes months ago, along with half a dozen records she had borrowed from friends and never returned.

Making a pile in the center of the room to box up later, she made her way to her sister's room. Unlike her door, Anais' was open and it appeared as though she was in the middle of collecting her belongings or the items strewn about were simply left over from their earlier abandonment of the home, but Anais was nowhere in sight. Eliza smiled to herself realizing her sister must have gone up to the attic to look for boxes and simply hadn't heard her calling. While she waited for her to return she decided to head into Helena's room to retrieve the journals.

Helena's room was in shambles, a result of their final day in residence. Eliza slowly made her way through the broken glass and the toppled furniture to the closet. Once again she encountered the remnants of Helena's rage. Every article of clothing had been ripped from its hanger and tossed to the floor; every box from the closet shelf had been torn open, its contents spilling onto the floor.

She had to clear a path just to get to the secret door at the back of the closet. Apparently forgotten, the room remained untouched, each item in its place. Eliza dropped down to her knees, preparing to enter the private chamber when she felt a firm hand grasp her shoulder.

"So you've found my honey hole, have you?" Helena spat.

Eliza spun around, coming face to face with her tormentor.

"What are you...Where...how did you?" Eliza stuttered, unable to form a sentence.

Helena let out a frightening cackle.

"What? You don't think that your mother's capable of convincing a panel of idiots it's time for her to go home?"

Eliz

a stared wide-eyed at the monster that called herself her mother.

"Speak, child, tell me, just what it is you're looking for. Wasn't the Book of Shadows enough?"

"I um...I was just...um"

Helena mocked her, repeating her words back in a childish voice. Eliza shrank back at the unexpected ridicule, forcing Helena further into the tiny space. Eliza's eyes darted around the room in search of anything she might use to protect herself, but Helena grabbed her by the jaw, compelling her to face her.

"Did you even grieve my absence or did you and your sister celebrate my incarceration? Don't bother answering. It doesn't matter now. I'm just going to ask you one more time. What are you looking for?"

Eliza swallowed hard, mustering up the courage to speak.

"I wanted Mercy's journals."

"Why?"

"So that I could study them. I know you're not a Lewis." Eliza hoped by changing the subject she could persuade Helena to let her have them.

"Ah, so the truth is finally out, is it?"

"Yes…no…only Anais and I know the truth. I promise we won't tell anyone."

"You promise, do you? And what good is a promise from a liar? Even if you shouted it from the rooftop it wouldn't matter. It never mattered."

Eliza tried to understand what it was she was saying but her words were far too cryptic for such a young girl to comprehend. Instead she focused her energy on a wire hanger just out of reach. If she could get to it, she might be able to use it as a weapon.

Using her newly acquired knowledge, she attempted to distract Helena. "Mercy Lewis was a liar. She lied to protect the coven."

Once again Helena laughed. "Of course she did; it was either that or hang. But that is no secret. By pointing the finger at George Burroughs she took the attention away from herself and the others. She was a hero to everyone in the sister-hood."

"Why would you want to share the name of a person that sent an innocent man to his death? Even Mercy felt bad about it."

"Don't you understand? Mercy Lewis, she betrayed a man she loved as a father, something no one else in the coven had the guts to do, at least until she made the claim. Her devotion to the coven was unparallel to any sister's actions during that dreadful time. Her name became synonymous with ruthlessness. It's that mercilessness that defined their coven and made people tremble with fear."

Helena released Eliza's chin from her grasp and looked into her eyes.

"That power will be mine again, of that I have no doubt. It's up to you whether or not you stand by my side or burn with the rest of them."

Armed now with a potential weapon, Eliza suddenly regained her confidence.

"Theona leads the coven now. The sisters have a new mission."

Helena's glare cut through Eliza like a sharp blade. "Theona won't be a problem. Let's just say she had a change of heart."

Eliza's skin crawled with the insinuation Helena might have done something to harm her.

"When you first saw me...you were going to ask how I got here. The doctors decided I was well enough to leave as long as I had someone to look after me. Who better to look after me than the woman that stole my children from me? She was more than willing to sign the papers and drive me out here when I promised to pack my bags and get out of town. She thought it would be best if I stayed away rather than under the same roof as my children. She even had the nerve to suggest I make myself scarce this afternoon while you and your sister retrieved your belonging."

Helena backed out of the closet and then smoothed out her clothes as if she was done with whatever business had brought her there, before continuing on.

"I had a different idea. When we arrived she was more than anxious to get me packed. The sooner she did, the sooner she could be rid of me. The awkward silence between us was making us both a bit jumpy. I suggested we have a cup of tea to settle our nerves and she graciously accepted. I couldn't help but notice how closely she watched me, as if she was afraid I might poison her. I'm no fool, Eliza. I know what people say about me, that I poisoned my husband, perhaps even my own parents. I have chosen to ignore all those rumors. Responding would only give them more credence and there would be no end to them. We sat at the kitchen table and I sipped my hot tea while she pretended to drink hers. She told me how well adjusted you girls were and how excited the coven was about the new direction they were going in. I smiled and nodded like the proper little host and she grew more comfortable. Perhaps she thought I was on some kind of medication. When I finished my tea I stood up and suggested we go up to my room to collect my belonging and she willing followed."

Eliza remained seated halfway between the closet and the secret chamber. Behind her back she twisted the hook of the hanger until it was completely unraveled.

"She had actually brought several empty boxes and went to retrieve them from her car. I used the opportunity to slip back into the kitchen and grab a chef's knife from the drawer. I even offered to help her carry the boxes up the stairs. We started boxing up my things when she realized the time had gotten away from her and she wanted to catch Anais before she headed over to the middle school to pick you up."

Eliza began to cry.

"Oh, don't worry, dear, your sister is fine."

"Theona?"

"Not so much I'm afraid. I asked her to help me get a box out of the attic before she left and she was more than willing to accommodate me. When we reached the top of the stairs I drove the knife into her back. She flailed around a bit, like a fish out of water. I was afraid I might have to stick her again, but she finally stopped. Did you know you could actually see the life drain out of a person's eyes when they die? It's quite amazing."

Eliza stared at her mother's emotionless face in shock. She was still clutching the hanger in her sweaty palm, but couldn't move.

"Where's Anais?" She whispered.

"Your sister's up in the attic with Theona. She wasn't very pleased with me when I drove over to the school to pick her up. I actually considered killing her too, but what would the fun be in that? I think it's time we join her, don't you?"

"If you hurt us they'll know you did it. They'll bring you back to the hospital."

"I have no intentions of hurting you or your sister. Now get up. It's time to join the others."

Eliza crawled on hands and knees to the doorway of the closet, carefully concealing the hanger inside her sleeve. If she had to, she would use it. Helena motioned for her to go first and she followed close behind.

At the top of the staircase, Eliza paused. She could hear her sister whimpering on the other side of the door.

Helena nudged her forward. The attic reeked of urine and she could clearly see her frightened sister's damp pants. She lay on her belly with her hands and legs bound behind her, her face only inches away from the deceased Theona. No attempt had been made to clean up the blood that saturated the bare floor. Theona's dead eyes stared straight ahead as if witnessing their ordeal even after the life was drained out of her.

Eliza trembled, fearing she might be the next victim if she couldn't get up the courage to stop Helena. As for Helena, she looked over her work with pride and satisfaction.

Eliza rushed to her sister's side, dropping down to her knees to brush her sister's hair away from her face.

"Your sister wanted to call the police when she saw what I had done to this traitor. She doesn't understand what's necessary to fulfill the destiny of our coven, but you do. Don't you, Eliza?"

"Let her go, Mother. We'll stay here with you if that's what you want. No one has to know what you've done."

Helena laughed. "Oh, Eliza, you're so naïve. If only it was that easy."

"But it is…it is that easy." Eliza pleaded.

"That's what your father said. Everything will be okay. No one will find out the truth and then he was gone and everything fell to pieces. There was no body to lie in the ground, no money in the bank. He wasn't gone twenty-four hours when the rumors started. I poisoned him they said. I poisoned my parents…my parents. Only I knew the truth, but what could I do. Admit that I was adopted, that I wasn't a Lewis. Admit my parents left me penniless in a broken-down home with a man who didn't love me? A man who only married me because of the power he thought I possessed. A man who realized too late he wed the wrong sister and wouldn't let a piece of paper stop him from fathering a child with her. Do you know what that does to a person? Do you have any idea what it's like to be raised by a woman who uses you like a lab rat?"

"Yes." Both Eliza and Helena turned at the unexpected response from the tearful teenager still bound on the floor. "Isn't it ironic that you have become everything you've tried to overcome?"

Helena shook her head, refusing to believe it was true. "No...I'm nothing like my so-called mother. She found pleasure in my pain. I only sought to teach you...to make you learn from your mistakes so you would become a better person."

Anais struggled to turn over so that she could face her abuser. Eliza came to her sister's aid, loosening the belt that bound her hands before moving down to her feet.

Helena watched in silence, trying to grasp what was happening. She no longer feared them running. It was clear they no longer feared her, in fact; it was almost as though they pitied her.

"Don't you dare look at me that way. I've only done what I had to in order to survive. I've been a prisoner in this house since the first day I arrived. I didn't have the memories of an innocent childhood to look back on. My childhood was filled with fear."

"What about ours?" Eliza screamed. "I was only six years old when you locked me in the attic so I wouldn't get in way of your coven's precious initiation ceremony. Do you have any idea how frightened I was? I could hear Anais' screams.

Then when I finally escaped and went downstairs to see if she was okay, you killed my pet right in front of me. What kind of lesson was I supposed to learn from that?"

"I didn't have a choice. I locked you up here to protect you from seeing something you were too young to understand. If your father had stuck around he might have taken you out somewhere for the evening. Your anger is misdirected. It's your father you should be angry at, not me."

"How could he protect me when you killed him?"

Helena dropped to the floor, exhausted. "I didn't kill your father, Eliza. He left me."

"You're a liar. You poisoned him."

"No...not that I didn't have every right after he betrayed me...but I didn't. He thought if it looked like he was sick and eventually died, it would be easier for me. I wouldn't have to face the shame of my husband walking out on me. I could continue to lead the coven without the disgrace of losing my husband to my own sister. He would go away and live his life and I would be the grieving widow, only it didn't happen that way. As soon as he was gone the rumors started. This is a small town, too small and everyone talks. They say the wife is always the last to know and it was certainly true in my case.

"Everyone had heard the rumors about your father and my sister. Some even suspected you were their love child. When he suddenly fell ill, which by the way was a complete fabrication, all eyes turned to me. My reputation didn't help matters. Of course, no one had the guts to come right out and ask me. The cowards just talked behind my back. Only those closest to me were brave enough to share the rumors."

"So why didn't you tell them the truth?" Eliza pressed.

"Because the rumors actually strengthened my command. Those that reported the rumors were rewarded for their loyalty and the others became easier to manipulate. If I had denied the rumors I would have lost my influence over them and my ability to lead."

"You're lying…Father wrote letters too us before he died. He would never leave us." Eliza cried.

Helena shook her head.

"That was all part of his plan. He knew eventually you would question his sudden death. Writing the letters was a way to speak to you from the grave. He was brilliant, I'll give him that."

"I don't believe you. He hid the letters so that you wouldn't find them. I only found them by accident."

"Clearly nothing I say will convince you of my innocence and I still have far more pressing matters to deal with right now."

Helena stood over her victim's body, lost in thought. Anais used the distraction to move her sister and herself away from Theona's lifeless body and toward the door.

"She used to be my friend, you know. She was one of my most trusted watchers. Her betrayal came as a great shock."Helena nudged the body with the toe of her shoe as though she expected some sort of response.

"It's a shame it had to end this way. There's only one thing I ask of those close to me…loyalty. Without loyalty there is nothing. Betrayal cannot go unpunished. Remember that, girls, and it will serve you well in the future. Once the bonds of trust are broken, you can't turn back. You have to accept the consequences for your actions. I have always made that one thing very clear. It was strange really… the look of shock on her face."

The girls huddled together at the threshold, too afraid to stay, yet unable to move. Anais held on to her sister like a mother bear protecting her cub. If necessary she would give her life to save Eliza. Suddenly, without provocation, Helena spun around to face her children.

Eliza clutched her fingers around the hanger still tucked inside her sleeve and pulled it free.

"Don't come near us or I swear I'll kill you." Eliza screamed.

Helena's eyes bulged with rage as she rushed toward the girls, her hands ready to grab them by the throat if necessary. In a split second, Anais pushed her sister out of harm's way just as her mother made contact, yanking out a handful of her beautiful hair. Anais screamed in pain before somehow managing to get free, ducking as Helena made another attempt to tackle her. Helena tried to stop herself, but lost her balance and tumbled down the stairs. A sickening snap echoed through the house as her head came in contact with the landing and her neck broke.

Anais helped Eliza to her feet, certain the worst was over.

Chapter Nineteen

In the all too familiar interrogation room of the police station, Eliza once again gave her statement to the detective while Anais was being questioned in a separate room down the hall. Unlike her sister who was having difficulty even speaking without bursting into tears and sobbing, Eliza appeared relaxed, if not comfortable. The young detective attributed her lack of emotions to shock, however the social worker on the other side of the glass wasn't so certain. Joan had seen her share of troubled teenagers in her time with the Office of Children and Family Services, but none with so little empathy for human life. She listened, making notes as Eliza conveyed the events leading up to her mother's death as if they were merely acts in a play she had seen. She shuddered at her cold, detached eyes that stared back at her through the glass. Did she know she was being watched or was she simply staring at her own reflection in the glass? The way she coldly described the sound of Helena's neck breaking was particularly quite disturbing. She equated it to the sound of a puppy being run over by a car rather than that of a branch snapping in a strong wind, like most would. Even the young officer looked back at the mirror to make sure the social worker caught it.

The interview was cut short when an older detective came into the room and whispered something to his younger partner. Both detectives left the room, as Eliza continued to stare at her image in the mirror. Joan made her way out to the hallway to see what was going on.

"We're going to have to call it a night. The older sister's a mess. Do you have somewhere the younger one can go for the night?"

"Yes, I've arranged for temporary foster care, but…I think she might need to be evaluated first."

The detectives nodded in agreement.

"We'll arrange for a separate rescue."

Joan returned to the viewing room where she watched the young girl casually examine a section of her unruly hair before releasing it into the tangled mess atop her head. Next she studied her fingernails as if she had received a manicure and was admiring the technician's work. There was something frightening about her behavior and it sent chills up her spine. Even if her story was true and she was the victim of years of abuse, she should be displaying some signs of emotion, whether it was sadness over the loss of her mother or relief that the abuse was over. The fact that she seemed unaffected by the violent confrontation almost to the point of boredom was extremely disturbing, especially when considering her older sister's reaction.

The ambulances arrived, one after another, first taking Anais who was displaying the most obvious signs of shock and then Eliza.

Joan followed the latter in her own car so that she could report her observations to the attending physician.

Eliza was wary, hesitant about going to the hospital, insisting her injuries were minor. It took the caseworker several minutes to convince her it was routine and that she would be in and out in no time. Eliza wasn't convinced, but didn't really have a choice in the matter since she was under-age.

The halls were eerily empty and Eliza couldn't help but feel a bit disappointed by the absence of supporters. It didn't occur to her that perhaps no one was yet aware of the tragedies that had taken place at the old Lewis home. Instead she told herself it was because everyone favored Anais. She imagined the sisterhood was probably all standing by her sister's bedside praying to their

Goddess for her speedy recovery. That was fine; Anais was weak and needed their support more than she did.

A young nurse appeared and handed Eliza a hospital gown to change into. The nervous smile on the nurse's face told her she was aware of the circumstances that had brought her there. As soon as Eliza changed, her clothes were placed in a plastic bag and taken away. A uniformed officer standing on the other side of the curtain whispered something to the nurse before taking the bag and leaving. It seemed peculiar that he would want her clothes and she called out to the nurse for an explanation. The nurse returned appearing more nervous than before.

"What is it, Dear?"

"Why did that officer take my clothes? What am I supposed to wear home?"

"He collected them for evidence. Whoever brings you home will bring you a change of clothes."

"Will I get them back?"

"Yes, I'm sure you will. The doctor will be in to see you shortly. Why don't you lie down and rest."

The nurse turned and left before Eliza had a chance to ask any more questions.

Eliza was about ready to get up and leave when a female doctor pulled the curtain aside and entered the room. Unlike the young nurse, the doctor wore an expression of warmth and concern. After a brief greeting she pulled a chair up beside the examining table.

"How are you feeling, Eliza?"

"I'm fine, I wasn't hurt at all. Can Anais and I go home?"

"Your sister needs to rest. She is having a little trouble processing everything that happened today. How about you? Is there anything you'd like to talk about?"

"I told the detective everything already."

"That's not really what I meant, Eliza. Would you like to talk about how you feel about your mother's death?"

"She's not my real mother."

"I wasn't aware…but she raised you, didn't she?" The doctor then flipped through the chart, annoyed that neither the police officers nor caseworker made mention of the important fact.

"I guess so. Can I go back home or do I have to stay somewhere else?"

"I'd like to talk a bit more, if that's okay."

Eliza shrugged.

"Was everything at home okay until today?"

"We weren't living there; we were staying at Theona's house."

"Yes, but before that…did you have a good relationship with your mother?"

"I told you…she's not my mother. I'd like to go now."

"I'm afraid you're going to have to stay a bit longer. If you'd like I can give you something to help you sleep."

Once again Eliza merely shrugged. She considered throwing a temper tantrum, but she didn't want anyone to think she was crazy like Helena. It was bad enough they continued to call the woman her mother, the last thing she wanted was for them to think that sort of thing ran in the family. Besides, it wasn't like she had any place to go. Clearly they wouldn't be returning to Theona's house and it didn't seem likely they could stay at their old house alone, so where did that leave them? What unfortunate sister was going to be burdened next?

After spending a restful night, Anais was ready to go home. While she was obviously very emotionally distraught over the loss of her mother and recent caregiver, the doctor felt she was stable enough to return home. While she, along with the coven, made burial arrangements for their fallen sisters, Eliza continued to be evaluated at the hospital. Finally, on the third day, with the coven putting pressure on the hospital administrators and against her doctor's wishes, she was released to her sister who had just turned eighteen.

The Coven

Joan was assigned as her caseworker and eagerly began the process of acclimating her and her sister to the system.

"I understand your mother hinted to the fact that your father was still alive. Do you have any idea where he might have gone if that was the case?"

"We were very young and, quite frankly, I think she was lying. If he did leave of his own free will, it's possible there might be some papers at the house that might give us a clue." Anais offered.

"What about the ticket? We found an unused train ticket to Boston with his papers. Maybe he's there." Eliza suggested.

Anais disagreed. "If he went to Boston, he would have used the ticket."

"Not if he left in a hurry. Maybe he didn't have time to get it so he just bought another one."

"That's as good a starting place as any. I know you girls would like to stay together, but the reality is you just can't survive on your part-time salary, and public assistance will only get you so far. It would be nice if you had family to help you out."

Anais nodded. The upkeep of the home itself was monumental. It had taken her and the sisters' days just to get the house in living order; she couldn't imagine what it would be like to maintain it. She had been lucky to have the sisterhood to rely on these past few days, but she couldn't expect them to continue to offer assistance. Nearly every window in the front of the house had to be replaced, not to mention the broken furniture that needed to be restored.

In the past few days she had come to realize her dream of going to college somewhere was no longer possible. With Eliza relying solely on her to see her through her remaining years in school, she would have to get a full-time job to support them. As much as she loved her little sister, the thought of spending the next four years looking out for her was overwhelming. Even on her best days, Eliza was a challenge. Anais just couldn't imagine what her high school years would be like. Then there was the matter of her coven. Anais was well aware of her extracurricular activities. While she didn't fear her turning into her mother, she still worried about her lack of empathy toward her peers.

Joan promised she would follow up on the Boston lead, though she thought it was a long shot. It seemed more likely the man was dead and buried in the back yard than living a secret life in Boston. The police had already run his license and Social Security number through their databases and come up empty. It was possible he was using an alias, but unless he wanted to be found, he most likely wouldn't be. Although she tried to distance herself from her cases, she couldn't help but feel bad for the girls. Even if Eliza turned out all right, Anais' life would never be the same. Not only did she have the daunting task of raising her teenage sister, but she would likely never find the time to continue school or maintain a relationship.

As the weeks passed, Eliza withdrew into a world not unlike that Helena had created for herself. She surrounded herself with her small group of loyal followers who were in awe of her Wiccan knowledge and eager to gain her approval. Their association with her alone was enough to put their classmates on notice and they no longer had to fear constant bullying and ridicule from the more popular students. The stigma attached to being the daughter, even if it wasn't biological, of a known murderer worked to her advantage. Those that had treated her badly in the past went out of their way to make amends.

Anais was too busy working and finishing up her senior year to notice any real changes in her sister. It was all she could do to put dinner on the table and provide her a safe place to come home to. The only time they spent together was across the dinner table and an occasional late movie night in front of the old black and white TV.

In the beginning, Joan checked in on the sisters twice a week. Finding the refrigerator stocked and the house in order, Anais soon convinced her they were doing well enough on their own. Despite her efforts she was no closer to locating the missing father and broadened her search to find any living relative.

"Are you sure there's no one else? A sibling or cousin of your father perhaps?"

"Not that I know of. My mother never spoke of any living family and I don't recall my father ever bringing anyone around. They were all very private people."

Anais promised to continue searching the house for any papers that might be helpful in the search. Satisfied with the stable environment she was providing for her sister, Joan agreed to reduce her visits to once a month.

Though deeply saddened by the murder of their new leader Theona, the sisterhood vowed to continue on in her name. After assisting Anais with arrangements for her mother's burial and then getting the house in order, the new coven sought to right the wrongs that Helena had been responsible for and invited the town to celebrate with them. Planning begun immediately, with a request to the city hall for a permit to have a bonfire at the town beach.

Happy they no longer had Helena to worry about, the council not only issued the permit, but also offered whatever assistance the coven might need in making the celebration successful.

The coven decided Theona would continue to hold the title of High Priestess posthumously until Sarah was old enough to take leadership. Until then, the sisterhood would be run as an equal partnership between its members, with everyone having a voice and decisions determined by vote. Under these guidelines the coven flourished like it never had before. Rather than fear and dread monopolizing their thoughts, they were able to focus on the task at hand. Instead of being attached to one role within the coven, the sisters were able to choose whatever task they wanted.

As the night of the big event drew closer, the community was all a buzz, anxious to see what the new coven had to offer. Even those residents who had fought hard to ban their religious rituals from public property admitted they were curious to see the new group in action. Posters announcing the celebration were plastered in every shop window and on telephone poll in town. Neither Anais nor Eliza could avoid questions about the coven, despite their attempt to distance themselves from everything related to Helena.

The week leading up to the celebration was particularly difficult as both the middle school and high school joined in the excitement with a spirit week. Students were encouraged to dress in their favorite costume honoring the town's most well known settlers. Local businesses offered up prizes for the best essay related to the town's history and ballots were handed out at the high school to elect the senior who would represent the school at the upcoming celebration.

Anais was particularly nervous that she would be selected for no other reason than out of some sort of misplaced guilt. "The last thing I want is to be paraded in front of the entire town while everyone whispers about how much I look like my mother and speculate as to whether or not I'm anything like her."

"Maybe you just won't be elected." Eliza offered, attempting to calm her sister's nerve.

"I wish I believed that, but you know as well as I do, this whole celebration is about making amends. Everybody in the coven wants to make up for all the misery Mother caused and everyone else feels guilty about turning a blind eye to our suffering. This is their way of making it up to us."

"So what if you are elected though? All you have to do is lead everyone from the meetinghouse to the beach, right? That's not all that bad."

Anais shook her head. Unlike her sister, who thrived on attention, she preferred to hide in the shadows. It was enough just to get through a normal school day with everyone's eyes on her, waiting for her to break down, how was she supposed to stand before a group of strangers?

"I suppose I could go to the organizers and ask them to take me out of the running."

Their conversation was cut short by a knock at the door.

"Are you expecting somebody?" Anais asked.

Eliza shook her head and headed to the door.

"Don't open it unless you know who it is."

Eliza peeked out the window and saw a girl about the same age as her sister.

"I think it's one of your friends."

Before Anais had a chance to respond, Eliza opened the door.

"Are you Eliza?" The young girl asked.

"Yes?"

"I'm supposed to give this to you." Handing her an envelope she turned and walked away, leaving Eliza standing alone at the threshold.

"What was that all about?" Anais asked, approaching her sister.

"I don't know. I guess it's a letter."

On the front of the plain white envelope was her handwritten name. Eliza turned it over before holding it up to the light. Unable to see through the envelope, she tore it open and then pulled out a single sheet of paper, folded in half. Written in the center of the page was one sentence.

I'll be waiting on the beach

"Who's it from?" Anais inquired.

"I have no idea. Maybe it's some sort of joke."

"If it is, I don't get it."

"Do you think it has something to do with the celebration?" Eliza asked nervously.

"I'm not sure, but it sounds like a threat. You're not going anywhere near the beach."

Eliza studied the note.

"Eliza? You're not going to the beach." Anais waited for a response. "Say it."

"Yeah, yeah…I'm not going to the beach."

Anais wasn't convinced. She knew her sister well enough to know as soon as she was told not to do something; she would make up her mind to do it, one way or another.

When the day of the celebration finally arrived, both Anais and Eliza rose early. Neither had slept much the night before so they went through the motions of getting ready for school in silence, both having too much on their mind for chitchat. Despite her worries, the Valedictorian, rather than Anais had been selected to represent the senior class at the evening's celebration and no one was happier about it than she. When they met in the kitchen for breakfast, Anais laid out the rules.

"After school I want you to come directly home. I want to be settled in before the celebration begins. Do you understand?"

Eliza rolled her eyes.

"I'm quite serious, Eliza. I don't want any excuses."

"I'll come directly home, I promise."

There was something about the look on her little sister's face that told Anais she was up to something, but when school let out Eliza kept her promise and went straight home.

To Anais' amazement, Eliza was upbeat rather than sulking as she had expected. She had anticipated an evening filled with endless requests to go to the celebration, but not once during dinner did she even mention it. Feeling guilty for suspecting she would break her word, Anais offered an alternative to a boring night at home watching the old black and white.

"If you'd like, you can go see a movie with one of your friends. I'm just going to be working on my senior project all evening."

Eliza smiled, grateful her sister had given her an excuse to go out. As long as she made sure no one saw her, she could watch the ceremony from a distance. An hour later Anais dropped her sister off at the local cinema, where her friend was waiting outside. They went inside and waited until Anais drove off before heading for the beach. The girls laughed at how easy it had been to fool Anais.

"We just have to be really careful no one sees us and tells her later. If she knows I lied to her, she'll never let me out again."

The girls made their way on foot, ducking behind buildings whenever they spotted headlights in the distance. Eliza's anticipation fueled her, giving her the strength to outrun her partner in crime. She had to stop several times for her friend to catch up, only making the journey seem longer. When they finally saw the flames of the bonfire in the distance, they slowed their pace, careful to remain in the shadows of the tall sea grass.

A huge bonfire was lit on the beach, and then everyone was encouraged to participate in a purification ritual. Members of the coven handed out slips of paper and asked that attendees write down any negative events they experienced at the hands of Helena. Once they had completed the task, they were instructed to toss the paper into the fire to cleanse themselves of any damaging energy that remained from their experiences.

At least a hundred residents had gathered for the ceremony, both young and old. The girls recognized teachers, shopkeepers, and the waitress from a popular clam shack as well as many of their classmates. Some seemed content to sit back and watch, while others stepped up to the fire to toss away their reminders of the woman that poisoned their community with her every action.

When the last paper had been tossed into the fire, the sisterhood asked them all to join hands. One by one they joined together until a circle was formed around the fire. Once again the elements showed their link to the coven as a stiff gust of wind ignited the flames, raising them up to the sky. An amalgamation of awes reverberated through the crowd in acknowledgement of the coven's power. Even Eliza felt the thrill of the moment. Some lingered, watching until the flames died down and nothing was left but the orange glow of embers.

Eliza's friend urged her to go.

"We've seen it, let's go. The movie will be letting out soon and Anais and my mother will be waiting for us."

"Just a couple more minutes. We still have plenty of time."

"Why? Everyone's going home. There's nothing left to see."

"There's a man down there sitting on that big rock."

"So…. come on."

"He looks like he's waiting for someone."

"So what, let's go. He's probably some creep hoping to see some of the witches go skinny dipping."

"I'll catch up. Go ahead."

Too afraid to get caught where she wasn't supposed to be and not wanting to argue, she turned and walked away.

Eliza waited until her friend had disappeared from sight before she carefully made her way closer to the man. She couldn't see him clearly in the darkness, but there was something about the man's posture that seemed familiar. She was too far away to see the details of his face, but his profile reminded her of her own. He appeared content to watch from a distance as though his celebration was separate from that of the others. He seemed hypnotized by the crackling wood and constant motion of the waves. It couldn't hurt to approach him. After all, if he was merely a stranger she could just walk away. She was less than twenty feet away when he finally turned to face her.

"I was wondering if you'd come." He said casually.

"Father? Is that you?"

"If you are Eliza."

"I am."

Eliza now stood in front of the man and though he was a bit older than she recalled, his hair graying around his ears; his features remained unchanged. He waited patiently while she studied him at length.

"Are you convinced I am who I say I am?" He asked.

Eliza nodded.

"Your sister? Is she well?"

"Anais, yes. She'll be graduating soon."

It seemed odd to be having such a normal conversation when she had so many questions to ask him. At the moment though, she couldn't come up with one.

"Did you find my letters?"

Eliza nodded, too enchanted by his presence to speak.

"What I said was mostly true. Despite the warnings from both my friends and family, I couldn't resist letting myself fall in love with her. She captured my heart the moment we met. I knew little of her family's history, only what she told me; which wasn't much. I grew up far enough away that I never heard any of the rumors about the Lewis women. We learned of the Wells connection to the Salem Witch Trials in our state history classes in grade school, but even if I'd have paid close attention, it wasn't likely I'd make the connection to her so many years later.

"I had friends that grew up in the area and warned me her mother had a reputation around town. Although witchcraft was never mentioned specifically, still they hinted that she seemed to possess powers that could make grown men weep and children run and hide at the mere sight of her.

I chalked it up to small town gossip and ignored their warnings. When I finally met the woman I could see how such rumors might gain credit. She was a tough old bat; stocky in build and just about the ugliest woman I'd ever seen. Her hair was a wiry mess pinned tightly into a bun at the top of her head and her face was a road map of wrinkles. Most of her teeth, at least those you could see; were stained yellow along with her fingers from years of heavy smoking. She dressed completely in black in dresses that looked like something out of the Victorian era and she walked with the use of a cane that I often found myself at the end of whenever I challenged her. She didn't like me any more than I liked her and she made no bones about telling me so every time I went to the old house to pick up Helena."

Eliza listened intently; amazed at just how accurate his description was to the portrait she had seen.

"We dated for nearly two years before I decided to pop the question and during those two years my friends did everything they could to try to discourage me from making, what they thought and I knew later was a big mistake. Since Helena wasn't fond of her mother, we rarely spent time at the old house and I convinced myself everything I had heard was nothing more than urban legend made up by people with little else to talk about. Wells wasn't anything like it is today; there were few places to go and little to do. There were very few transplants so the majority of the town was made up of lifelong residents. History has a way of changing over time when the well is dry and the same stories are passed down from generation to generation.

"By the time I got my nerve up enough to ask her to marry me, my parents had been drawn into the pool of rumormongers, having heard the endless accounts of Helena's family's dastardly deeds. My father threatened to remove me from his will if I went through with the marriage and my mother broke down in tears every time we spoke. Finally, we decided it would be best for everyone if we simply eloped, sparing our families from having to meet and whatever might come as a result of their differences. I loved my parents dearly, but I loved Helena more.

"In the beginning, everything was just about wonderful, or at least as wonderful as it could be living under the same roof as her parents. We respected each other's privacy and tried to stay out of each other's way as much as possible. At the time, her mother was very secretive about her affiliation with the coven and I never witnessed anything that made me believe the rumors had any basis of truth to them. Helena spoke little about her mother and when she did speak, it was nothing related to witchcraft. She insinuated that there had been some abuse during her childhood, but when I asked her to be more specific, she shut down. Without any insight as to what her mother might have done, I couldn't help her.

"We were only married a short time – Anais was only three – when her parents died. Back then I had no reason to question her, so when she told me they died from food poisoning, I believed her. We often ate separately to avoid conflicts, so it was plausible that they might have eaten tainted meat or canned goods that neither Helena nor I consumed. They were buried quickly, with only a small group in attendance, but again I thought little of it considering the woman's reputation.

"It was shortly after that when I started to notice a change in Helena. Out of nowhere she started reading everything she could get her hands on related to witchcraft. She neglected Anais and the house to spend hours practicing spells. I didn't know just what to do. I confronted her when I overheard her talking on the phone to one of her mother's friends, planning what sounded like some sort of ceremony. At first she denied it all, telling me I heard wrong, but when I pressed she admitted the rumors I'd heard were true. I felt like a fool. All my friends had tried to warn me and I hadn't listened. I begged her to stop before she got in too deep, but the more I implored her to stop, the more she dug her heels in. That was when I turned to her sister.

"She had always been kind to me, even when everyone close to her was against me. I had nothing to lose by reaching out to her. The worst she could do was tell Helena and so what if she did, I had nothing to hide. Helena no longer cared about anything but the coven. I don't think the women had any idea when they made her their new leader what she would become. To this day I believe that they elected her out of guilt for the way they had treated her during her mother's reign.

"Your mother and I met several times to try to come up with a solution. Neither of us intended to fall in love at all, and certainly not under the circumstances that brought us together. Our love was born out of our mutual concern for Helena's mental health. We never dreamed our frustrations over our inability to persuade Helena into seeking help would force us into a position that allowed us the opportunity to get to know each other on a very different level than a brother and sister-in-law should.

"Your conception, like everything else; was a surprise to us and we weren't prepared for the consequences of our actions. When it became apparent that your mother was pregnant, Helena began to question her. In a town as small as Wells nothing gets past the coven. We had been spotted having coffee at the local diner. It wasn't like we were trying to hide our friendship, so we often met in public. Foolishly perhaps, we didn't think any-one would pay much attention to us. We sat on opposites sides of a booth, conversing over coffee and sometimes a piece of pie. It was all so very innocent. It was only when we were alone that things became passionate and even then it seemed completely natural. Neither one of us felt any guilt since Helena cared about nothing but the coven.

"When the rumors and speculations made their way to Helena, she brushed them all off as nothing more than her sister challenging her authority by making her seem vulnerable. When the baby arrived, however, Helena felt pressured to claim the role of mother to save her reputation in the community. She was afraid that she would become a laughing stock if anyone found out the truth. Your mother spent the last few months of her pregnancy in hiding, away from prying eyes. Only the three of us knew the truth. She suffered with bouts of fever and sickness through the final trimester of her pregnancy. Despite the fact that Helena never gained any weight, the coven accepted her word that you were her child. If they thought otherwise, they were smart enough to keep it to themselves. Although the delivery was a difficult one, your mother delivered you on her own, with only Helena and myself by her side. A few moments after your first breath, she took her last. As I said in my letter, I believe Helena was somehow someway responsible for your real mother's passing.

"In that moment my life as I knew it was shattered. On the one hand I had you, a precious reminder of what I shared with your mother. On the other hand, I had a spiteful wife that could never forgive my infidelity. Never once did she consider it was her actions that drove me into the arms of her sister. I was left alone to pick up the pieces and bury the woman I had grown to love.

"Helena publicly went through the motions of being the grieving sister, yet all the while she was celebrating her death behind closed door. It sickened me to be in the same room with her.

"I hoped that in time Helena would come to love you as her own, but her resentment only grew and I couldn't stand by and watch her destroy our family any longer. The older you got, the more you resembled your mother and became a constant reminder of our betrayal. I couldn't bear to watch her pit you against your sister, but I had no way to stop her either. Helena's connections were far greater than I ever imagined. Everywhere I went I was turned away, lawyers, police, they were all too scared to go up against her. She had built a fortress, surrounding herself with individuals that would do whatever she asked.

I went to Child Services to file a case of abuse against her, but nothing ever came of it. When a month passed with no action I returned to the agency to find there was not a record of my previous visit. Every time you appeared ill, I brought you to the doctor, hoping that she might confirm what I suspected, that you were being slowly poisoned; but again nothing came of the visits.

"I thought if I left town and built a new life for myself I could petition the court for custody. I found a small apartment on the south side of Boston. It wasn't much to look at and was barely furnished, but it served my needs. I found a job, nothing great but it paid the rent, put food in my mouth and I was able to set a little aside each week for a legal fund. It wasn't until I tried to hire a lawyer that I realized her reputation traveled far beyond the borders of Wells. The ink wasn't even dry on the papers when she threatened my lawyer and his family. Gifts of dead animals began to arrive on his doorsteps, and his children were followed to and from school. He quickly dropped me as a client. Every time I thought I'd found a new one, either word from their fellow colleagues or local covens would scare them off.

"Finally I gave up, settling for letters from friends back home who would keep me informed of her activities and the health of you and your sister. I could never be sure whether or not the contents of their letters were true or if Helena had threatened them as well. I could only pray their loyalties were with me, since I had never given them any reason to dislike me.

"The years passed slowly for me in Boston while I tried unsuccessfully to build a new life. I dated a handful of women, but would never allow myself to become too attached to anyone. Like I said, my heart was shattered the day I lost your mother and no one could replace her or the love I found with her. When I wasn't working, I spent hours at the library reading everything I could get my hands on regarding the Salem Witch Trials and the Lewis family, but all my research was for naught.

"I came to see I would never actually be free of Helena. Not really. I could travel to the ends of the earth and she would still find me. Every loan I applied for was turned down, every job I got, I eventually lost. No explanations were ever given to me. Not that I needed any. I knew somehow Helena was responsible. She was committed to seeing my life was a living hell and no matter what it took she was prepared to do it.

"Every year that passed and I didn't have my children with me was another notch in her belt. It was torment. I was willing to do anything to have you and your sister back in my life. Every year on the anniversary of your mother's death...your birthday, I traveled to Wells. I would travel at night under the clock of darkness, then ditching my car in the cornfields. I walked along the back roads, ducking for cover each time I saw headlights for fear I would be spotted. When I finally reached the bottom of the driveway, I crawled on my hands and knees through the tall grass to the old shed. If anyone had seen me, they would have thought I lost my mind. In the early morning when you woke and turned on your bedroom light, the very sight of you in your window comforted me. It was enough for me to know you were still alive, that she hadn't taken her hatred for me and her sister out on you.

"I'm not sure exactly when, but at some point I realized someone was visiting the shed. Things were moved and the stagnant air seemed somehow fresher despite the dust and debris left behind. I considered leaving a message in hopes it was you, but I couldn't be certain Helena wouldn't find it.

"I watched as you left the house for school, wishing I had the nerve to call out your name, but I never did. I would sleep all day waiting for you to come home so that I could see you one more time before nightfall came and I left once more. The weeks that followed my annual visits were particularly difficult. It was as if I tore open an old wound that had just begun to heal. Each year I told myself I would never do it again, but then I'd find myself counting down the days to my next visit.

"When word finally came to me that Helena had died, it was all I could do to stop myself from driving straight home. My friends were generous in the details of her passing and I knew I had to keep my distance. They warned that my sudden appearance might cause doubt on the statements you and your sister gave and that I might then find myself accused of murder. I trusted that they would tell me when the time would be right, so I waited. Every day I collected my mail and prayed for a letter. Finally, word came about the coven's announcement of a celebration.

"The new sisterhood was the answer to my prayers. It meant that I no longer had to fear any retaliation from Helena's underlings. They had a new mission, one of peace and harmony, not pain and misery. Most surprising of all was the fact that it was them and not my friends who sent me the message it was time to come home.

"I can't begin to explain to you just how overjoyed I was. It was everything I had worked for, prayed for and dared to hope for. To finally be a family once again was a greater gift than I'd ever received."

Choking back tears, he waited for Eliza's response. He had rehearsed every scenario in his mind a thousand times. Would she spit in his face and tell him she never wanted to see him again or wrap her arms around him in a long overdue embrace? Several minutes passed in complete silence, only interrupted by the sound of the surf and the occasional cries of a seagull soaring overhead. Finally she placed her hands over his and stared into his eyes.

"I knew you'd come home someday."

That was it. She didn't rush into his arms like he'd envisioned or turn her back and walk away. She didn't ask for explanations or challenge what he said. She simply stated what she'd felt all along; that eventually he would come home to her. Somehow, despite everything Helena had done, after all these years, he came home. Not as she'd imagined, with a knock at the front door, but as a distant figure atop a rock. A silhouette against the backdrop of a starry night, somehow familiar yet still a stranger.

Continue the journey with *The Coven*'s sequel:
The Witches of Wells

Prologue

Salem Massachusetts
Gallows Hill
July 22, 1994

Cloaked in darkness, with only the light of the full moon to guide them, the candidate and her sponsor move silently up the embankment. The air was thick with thousands of unseen insects swarming the hillside, drowning out the sounds of modern day life and transporting them back in time. What was once a grassy slope was now a steep ledge of bedrock unearthed to make way for the railroad built in the early 19th century. Beyond the rock they ascended a recently cleared path through a cluster of twisted vines and thorny bushes where another member of the coven meets them, wielding a sword.

"Who comes to this sacred place?"

"I am Ingrid, spawn of the earth and the heavens."

"Who speaks for you?"

"It is I, Radiance, who vouches for her."

"You are entering a place of power, a place beyond imagining. As you step between the worlds, you stand on the threshold of the eternal life, are you strong enough?"

"I am."

"Then prepare for your rebirth."

Stepping forward, the challenger draws her sword, cutting the tie that connects Ingrid's robe. As her sponsor removes the robe, exposing her naked body, the challenger steps closer, placing a blindfold over her eyes. From the darkness, the remaining members of the coven move forward to surround the candidate. Truly at the mercy of those around her, she allows them to lead her down the path in silence. Without her sight, she relies on her other senses to comfort her. The smell of burning wood permeates the air, though she isn't close enough to feel its heat. As they come to a stop she hears the sound of liquid being poured into a vessel and she remains still. Guided by the others, she steps into a shallow basin where she is bathed in preparation of the ceremony. One at a time, each member of the coven steps forward to participate in the bathing ritual until she is believed to be cleansed of her previous life before being dried off. Once dry, a long white robe, representing her purity is draped over her body and she is led to the fire circle.

Stepping out of the darkness, dressed in a long black cloak, the High Priestess approached the candidate.

"Have you come to us of your own free will?"

"I have."

"Are you willing to suffer to prove your commitment?"

"I am."

Removing her blindfold, the High Priestess takes her hand, directing her to kneel before her. Stepping forward, the challenger bows before their leader as she presents the sword. Accepting the instrument, the Priestess turns the candidates palm upward, pressing the blade into the heel of her hand to extract a small amount of blood before pressing it against her heart.

"Repeat after me... I solemnly swear to protect and defend my sisters of the coven. I vow to never reveal any secrets within the coven. I swear on my mother's womb and my eternal life, and in the presence of those before me."

Repeating the vow, Ingrid rose with the help of her sponsor.

"Come and be anointed."

Without hesitation, Ingrid stepped forward. Removing a vial from the pocket of her robe, the Priestess spills the oil into a waiting vessel.

Dipping her finger into the oil, she traces the sign of the pentacle upon Ingrid's forehead.

"You have been accepted into the coven. I name you Summer in honor of this sacred season."

With that, the women of the coven clasp their hands as a sign to unity and rebirth. Making a circle around the fire they began to chant.

Just beyond the rocky slope, where the path branched out, leading to the plateau and the secret ceremony playing out before him, a young boy crouches behind a bush.

Like so many nights before, the pretty lady didn't arrive until well after his mother had thought him asleep. It started a few weeks before school ended. His bedtime had always been eight o'clock, then without even telling him why, his mother told him he had to go to bed at seven. Not only did all his friends get to stay up much later, but it was way too light out to fall asleep. Although she told him he could read in bed until he got tired, that wasn't the point. While he was stuck in bed, his friends were all playing outside just down the street. He knew they were probably laughing at him, calling him a baby. It wasn't long before they were making plans without him and by the time school was out, they had their summer already planned and their plans didn't include him.

He tried to explain to his mother that he was too old for such a baby bedtime, but she wouldn't listen so he decided he would just stay awake until she went to bed just to show her how grown up he was. Most nights he fell asleep before she came in to check on him around eight, but the nights the pretty lady came over she forgot all about him. On those nights, he was too curious to fall asleep.

Before the lady came over he could hear his mother pacing the floors. Some nights he could hear her pray, asking God for guidance. The fear in her voice scared him. He wasn't sure what she was so afraid of because as soon as the pretty lady arrived she seemed to be fine.

Most nights he would lie on the floor, peering under the door to see down the hall into the living room. That's how he knew what the lady looked like. She always wore long dresses and sandals on her feet. They sat on the floor instead of the couch, which he thought was funny. He had never seen grownups sit on the floor like that. While his mother's purse only had boring stuff aside from the occasional pack of gum, the pretty lady's bag seemed to be filled with all sorts of interesting things. Every time she came, she seemed to have something different in her bag.

There were candles that she lit and placed on the floor between her and his mother as well as small bags filled with what looked like dead grass. She had a bunch of weeds that she would light and then blow out before dancing around the room with them. He hated that one. It smelt really gross and he had to cover his mouth and nose so he wouldn't cough and give himself away. His favorite thing was a cool purple crystal that hung from a chain. When she took that out of her bag, he simply had to get a closer look at it.

Pulling himself off the floor, he carefully opened his bedroom door; listening to make sure they hadn't heard him. Silently he made his way down the dark hallway toward the living room on his tiptoes. Dropping to his hands and knees behind the back of the sofa, he watched as the lady dangled the chain over a drawing of a star. While his mother's eyes were closed, the lady looked down at the drawing and whispered a rhyme he wasn't familiar with. Every nerve in his body tingled in anticipation. He had never seen anything like this and he wondered if all grownups played this game when their kids went to bed. When the crystal stopped spinning, the lady told his mother they were done. While she gathered her things and his mother walked her to the door, he slipped back into his room and into his bed.

He thought about asking his mother who the lady was and why he couldn't stay up and play with them, but he was afraid if he admitted he was awake she would only put him to bed earlier. He was almost eight and a half and she still treated him like a baby. If he had a dad he was sure he would let him stay up later. Sometimes, when he was mad at his mother, he told her he wished he had a dad like his friends. He knew it hurt her feelings and he always said he was sorry later.

She never got mad at him when he said it, she would only cry, promising him that when he was older she would tell him about his father.

As the weeks passed, the lady came more and more. Each time she came, his mother seemed more and more nervous. Finally, his mother told him they would be going on a trip. He was so excited. Every summer his friends went on family vacations while he was stuck at home. His mother always promised they would go away someday, but it never happened. Maybe he was finally going to get to go to the big amusement park he had heard his friends talk about, the one with the big roller coasters and scary rides.

Finally, on the day they were set to leave, she explained they were going to Massachusetts. At first he was disappointed but then she explained that they would visit some of the museums he had heard about and go on a boat ride, so he was more excited. They had spent the last three days, doing just that and he was even allowed to stay up as late as he wanted. He had almost forgotten about the pretty lady and her games when his mother suddenly announced he had to go to bed early their final night in town. Despite arguing that he could sleep in the car the following day, she insisted he turn in at eight o'clock. Although it was an hour later than she allowed at home, it was still too early and he struggled to fall asleep while she sat outside their motel room on a plastic chair, writing in her journal.

Occasionally he would sneak out of bed and peek through the big window to see what she was doing, but her head remained bent while she wrote in the leather book. He was just starting to doze off when a car pulled into the lot shining its bright headlights into the room. Moments later, his mother and the pretty lady entered the room and he watched through his squinted eyes across the darkened room as his mother removed her clothes and wrapped herself in a long robe. As she approached the bed, he closed his eyes and held his breath while she leaned in to kiss his forehead.

As quietly as she'd come the pretty lady, followed by his mother, slipped out the door and got into her waiting car. Jumping out of the bed, he peered through the curtains as he watched the car disappear down the road. Stripping off his pajamas, he quickly dressed in a t-shirt and shorts before pulling his sneakers onto his bare feet. Peeking out the window once more to make sure no one was watching, he opened the door and sprinted for the road.

He ran until his stomach hurt and had nearly given up hope of finding them, when he spotted the familiar car. Stopping long enough to catch his breath, he scanned the area for any sign of movement. Other than the moon, there was no light in the immediate area and he nervously considered turning around and heading back to the motel. Steadying his breath he listened for any other sounds besides the chirping crickets and humming insects. Across the dark street, beyond an embankment, he could smell burning wood. Cautiously he crossed the street, making sure to look both ways like his mother had taught him. The hill was more difficult to climb than he had expected and it took him several minutes to reach the top. Moving quickly down the path, he stumbled on roots and rocks, scrapping his hands and knees in the process. Finally he arrived at the stage where several women, including his mother were dancing around a fire.

Ducking behind a large rock, he watched in fascination while the women moved around the crackling fire. Coming to an abrupt stop, all but one woman knelt down with their backs to the flames. While the woman in the black robe disappeared into the darkness, the women swayed back in forth with their eyes closed. Finally the woman returned with a bowl in her hands. As he watched from afar, she dipped her fingers into the bowl and wrote something on each of the women's foreheads. As she did so, one at a time the women began to rise until only his mother remained kneeling. With the help of two women, one on each side, she was helped to her feet while her eyes remained closed.

Unable to hear what was being said, he moved in closer, careful not to give himself away. He watched as his mother leaned her head backward toward the fire and the remaining liquid was poured over her forehead. In an instant, flames shot up, causing the two women to let go of his mother as they stepped out of harm's way. Unable to steady herself, she stumbled backward into the flames and he watched in horror as the white gown ignited, engulfing her in flames. While the women scrambled to free her from the fire, she screamed in agony as the oils she was anointed with only fueled the fire. Powerless, he stood, unable to move, as he watched his mother be consumed by the fire. A warm stream of release spread across the front of his shorts and down his legs as he looked on in horror.

Removing their cloaks, the women quickly surrounded Ingrid and quickly began smothering the flames. When they finally stepped back, removing the last cloak from her blistered body, all that remained was the look of terror on her melted face. Someone began to scream and it wasn't until the group moved in his direction that he realized it was he. Unable to cope with what he had witnessed, he withdrew from reality into a world of his own making. It would be several years before he would be able to rejoin society without the paralyzing fear that held him captive in his self-imposed prison.

The Witches of Wells

Other books by
Cheryl Kennedy

Buried Secrets
The Fatal Cache
The Forgotten Treaty